MARY CAMDEN HAD
A GOOD REASON TO BE UPSET.

It was Christmas Eve and, unlike the rest of her family, she wasn't in Glenoak. Nor was she curled up in a warm bed or roasting chestnuts on an open fire. Mary was stranded in the Chicago airport. Alone. Waiting in an endless line of angry travelers. Just her luck.

She took a deep breath and looked out the giant windows of the airline terminal. When her flight from Buffalo had landed, the snow was light, but now a massive blizzard swirled so thick that even the blinking red lights of the runway had been erased from view. All flights were now canceled—including her connecting flight to Los Angeles. Was there any way to get home on a night like this?

DON'T MISS THESE
7th Heaven™
BOOKS!

AND COMING SOON

7th Heaven™

LUCY'S ANGEL

by Amanda Christie

An Original Novel

Based on the hit TV series
created by Brenda Hampton

Random House 🏠 New York

www.randomhouse.com/teens

Library of Congress Control Number: 2001092376
ISBN: 0-375-81419-1

Printed in the United States of America
First Edition
October 2001
10 9 8 7 6 5 4 3 2 1

7th Heaven™

LUCY'S ANGEL

LUCY'S ANGEL

ONE

"Did you check over here?" Lucy asked.

Simon was rummaging through a box on the other side of the attic. "Not yet," he said.

Squatting down to avoid the low ceiling, Lucy opened another box. She and Simon were in their grandfather's attic, looking for a Christmas tree skirt. That morning, the four of them—Lucy, Simon, Grandpa, and his wife, Ginger—had bought a tree. They'd spent most of the day decorating it. Now all it needed was a skirt to cover the stand.

Lucy hummed as she looked through the box. She was glad she and Simon had decided to spend some of their Christmas vacation with Grandpa and Ginger. The siblings had driven down to Phoenix, Arizona, a few days ago.

But Lucy was eager to get back home, too. Tomorrow was Christmas Eve. By the time Lucy and Simon returned to Glenoak, Mary and Matt would be home. Lucy always looked forward to the holiday season as a time to spend with her brothers and sisters.

Plus, she and Simon would be back just in time for the church's annual Christmas Eve party. Lucy was looking forward to the caroling, especially the solos she would be singing!

On the other side of the attic, Simon sighed. "How come Grandpa doesn't know where the tree skirt is? All the heat from downstairs seems to have escaped up here to the attic, and I'm *hot!*"

"I don't know," she said. "I guess Ginger couldn't find it."

Their grandfather depended on Ginger to do things like climbing around in the attic. Although he was still pretty fit, he suffered from Alzheimer's disease. Sometimes it was hard for him to keep track of what he was doing.

Simon closed a box and sat back on his heels. He wiped his forehead with the back of his hand. "Well, I don't know where it could be," he said. "We've been up here for over an hour. I feel like my nose is permanently clogged with dust!"

Lucy smiled. Despite his complaints, she knew Simon was having a good time. The last few days with Grandpa and Ginger had been wonderful. Spending an hour in the attic looking through boxes was a minor inconvenience.

Lucy tucked a strand of hair under the bandanna she was wearing and closed the last box.

"Did we miss anything?" she asked, looking around for boxes they hadn't opened. Over the last hour, they'd discovered lots of interesting things—toys, clothes, ancient newspapers. Lucy wondered if anything they'd found had belonged to their mother. After all, this was the house she'd grown up in.

"I don't think so," Simon said. He rubbed his forehead again, then exploded with a sneeze. "Let's get out of here," he said, sniffing.

"Wait a minute," Lucy said. In a far

corner of the attic was a small box she hadn't noticed before. Ducking her head even lower, she crawled back to it.

"Where are you going now?" complained Simon.

"There's one more," Lucy said.

This last box was old, older than the others they'd already looked through. And it was smaller, too.

How long has this *been here?* Lucy wondered. She felt a flicker of excitement as she lifted the top.

But except for a ball of crumpled yellow newspaper, the little box was empty. *What was I expecting?* she thought with a shrug. *A treasure map? Priceless jewelry?*

Lucy shook her head. It *was* hot. And dusty. She and Simon would go downstairs and report that they couldn't find the skirt. Maybe they could go out tonight or early tomorrow and buy a new one.

She was closing the box when something caught her eye. Afterward, she couldn't say exactly what it was. It was as if a door had opened to let through a flash of brilliant light and then closed again.

Whatever it was, it had come from the bottom of the box.

Puzzled, Lucy reached down and picked up the crumpled newspaper. There was something wrapped in it!

"Hey!" Simon suddenly shouted from the other side of the attic. "I found it! It was right under my nose the whole time!"

Lucy glanced up to see Simon waving the tree skirt triumphantly. Then, slowly, carefully, she unwrapped the newspaper in the little box.

"Lucy?" Simon called. "Hello?"

The first thing Lucy saw was a gleam of gold, and then a creamy white. The newspaper fell away, and Lucy was holding a precious figurine made of porcelain. It was an angel—a cherub—with gold-painted wings and golden hair. At the top of the figure was a loop of cloth. Lucy guessed it had been made as a Christmas tree ornament.

"Beautiful," she whispered, turning the angel over in her hands. She didn't know anything about porcelain figurines, but this one seemed exquisitely made. It was well balanced, seamless, and perfectly painted.

Simon walked across the attic and crouched next to Lucy. He peered over her shoulder at the figurine.

"Where'd you find that?" he asked.

"In this box," Lucy said, still cradling the cherub in her hands. She had the strangest feeling—as if the angel had been waiting in that box for many years, waiting just for her.

"It's beautiful," Simon said. He reached out a finger and stroked a perfect wing.

Lucy noticed the tree skirt, hanging forgotten from Simon's other hand.

"Where did you find it?" she asked.

"It was *underneath* one of the boxes. I never thought to look there. I just happened to see one corner sticking out."

"Good job, little bro," Lucy said.

Simon grimaced. "Gee, thanks a lot, big sis."

Lucy grinned. Simon was growing up, but that just made it more fun to tease him about being younger than her. He *really* hated it now.

Simon took the figurine from her for a closer look.

"Hey," he said. "Look at this!"

He showed her the bottom of the figurine. There, scrawled in green marker, was a single word. It was a name.

Lucy.

Lucy gasped.

Simon put his hand on her shoulder. Whether it was to steady her or himself, she didn't know.

They looked at each other.

"Time to show this stuff to Grandpa," Simon said.

Lucy nodded. Together, they crawled over to the steps and started down.

TWO

Grandpa and Ginger were sitting in the family room, talking and listening to Christmas carols. The Christmas tree stood in front of the picture window, shining with lights and ornaments.

"Any luck?" Ginger asked Simon and Lucy as they walked in.

Simon held up the tree skirt.

"Bravo!" Grandpa said. "I knew it was up there somewhere. Quick, let's put it around the base of the tree and cover up that ugly stand."

Grandpa and Simon got down under the tree and started arranging the skirt.

Ginger smiled at Lucy. "Honey, you're

covered with dust." Then she noticed the box Lucy held in her hands. "What have you got there?" she asked.

"I found something," Lucy said.

"Huh?" Grandpa called from under the tree. "What's that?"

"I found something, Grandpa," Lucy repeated. "I thought maybe you'd know what it is."

Grandpa crawled out from under the tree. "Well, let's see it," he said.

He took the box from Lucy and sat down. When he opened the box and saw what was inside, he froze, a look of wonder on his face.

"Honey, where did you find this?" he asked quietly.

"In that box," Lucy said. "It was pushed way back under the eaves. I almost didn't see it. Grandpa, what is it?"

Slowly, Grandpa reached into the box and lifted out the angel. "I can't believe it," he said.

Simon and Ginger drew close to look.

"It's beautiful," Ginger said reverently.

Grandpa shook his head. "I thought

this was lost forever. Where did you say you found it?" he asked.

Lucy told him again. "And Grandpa," she said. "*My name* is written on the bottom!"

Grandpa turned the figure over and smiled. "Oh, yes. I'd almost forgotten about that."

"You mean you know about it?" Lucy asked.

"Well of course I do!" Grandpa said. "Your mother put it there."

"She did?" Simon asked.

Grandpa nodded. He passed the angel to Ginger, who handled it gently, admiring the fine craftsmanship.

"Your mother must have written that name on the bottom of that ornament when she was . . . oh, I don't know, six or seven years old. You know that Lucy was always one of her favorite names?"

Lucy felt a slow blush of pleasure. She shook her head. "I didn't know that."

"Oh, yes," Grandpa said, settling back into his chair. "Let's see. . . . It must have been about thirty-five years ago. Like I said, when your mother was only six or seven years old.

"It was just about this time of year, a couple of days before Christmas. The weather was just horrible!"

Ginger set the figurine on the little desk next to Grandpa's chair and disappeared into the kitchen. Lucy and Simon sat down on the floor to listen.

"I remember I was sitting right here, worried sick," Grandpa continued. "Annie—your mother—and *her* mother were out running errands when this thunderstorm hit. It came out of nowhere! Wasn't on any of the weather reports. Fierce winds, hail, rain so hard you couldn't see your hand in front of your face. Annie and her mother were caught out in it, and I was stuck here."

"That must have been tough, Grandpa," Simon said.

"It was terrible," said Grandpa. "It's a terrible feeling not being able to do anything when your loved ones are in danger. I sat by the phone and stared out that very window.

"I prayed and I sang Christmas songs, hoping that somehow that would help. I didn't know it then, but your grandmother told me later that she and Annie were doing the very same thing. . . ."

"Which one do you want to sing next?"
Annie's mother asked. She glanced down at
her daughter and smiled.

Annie was sitting next to her mom in
the front seat. Outside, the rain was thun-
dering down around them. It was dark, but
the glow of the dashboard lights was cozy.
Annie felt snug and safe.

"'Hark! The Herald Angels Sing'?" Annie
asked.

"Okay," said her mom. She was holding
the wheel with both hands and squinting
through the windshield. "Sure is raining,"
she said.

Annie nodded.

"Well," her mother said. "As long as we
creep along nice and slow, we'll be fine.
You're not worried, are you?"

"No," Annie said.

"Good," said her mom. "Then I'm not,
either. Ready to sing?"

Annie nodded.

"Here we go!" said her mom. "Hark! The
herald angels sing, 'Glory to the newborn
king!'"

Suddenly bright light filled the car. Annie's mom gasped as a sixteen-wheeled truck roared past.

Annie felt a strange, floating sensation as the car spun in a slow circle. Beside her, Annie's mom turned the wheel one way, then the other, trying to regain control.

The next thing Annie knew, the car lurched, then pitched forward. With a soft <u>crunch</u>, it came to a stop.

"Honey, are you okay?" asked Annie's mother quickly.

Annie nodded. "I think so," she said. "What happened?"

"The car spun around," she said. She peered out her window. "We slid off the road."

"Oh," Annie said. She thought for a second. "How do we get back <u>on</u> the road?"

"I don't know, honey," she said. "We may be stuck here for a while. Why don't you sit tight, and I'll get out and look around?"

"No, Mommy!" Annie said. "I don't want you to go outside!"

Her mom paused, then looked out the window. "Well, it is pretty wet out there," she said. "What do you want to do?"

"Sing?" Annie asked.

Her mom smiled. She flicked on the hazard lights and said, "Okay. Ready?"

And they sang. And while they sang, a second light came up behind them, but so gradually that for a long time neither of them noticed. Finally, Annie's mom saw the gleam in her rearview mirror, growing steadily stronger.

"Honey," Annie's mom said, "there's a car coming. The people inside might be able to help us, but I need to be sure they see us, so I'm going to get out. Okay?"

Annie didn't like the idea of being in the car alone, but what her mother said made sense. "Okay," she agreed.

Annie's mom gave her a kiss. "I'll be right back," she said.

Gathering her coat around her, she opened the car door and stepped out into the rain. When she closed the door, Annie was alone. She hummed "Hark! The Herald Angels Sing" and tried to wait patiently.

She saw the light her mom had noticed, behind them on the road. She watched it get closer and closer, until it stopped behind them. Before long, the door was *opening again, and her mom was peering in at her.*

"We're in luck!" she said. "Come on, kiddo. We're going home in style!"

Annie took her mom's hand and slid across the seat. Outside, the rain was coming down in buckets. On the road, Annie could see the shadowy shape of a large truck.

"Come on, honey!" her mom said, helping her up the small embankment to the road. "Let's get out of this rain!"

They climbed to the truck. When they got closer, Annie could see that it was a tow truck. She could just make out the shape of a large man bent over behind the truck.

Her mom opened the passenger-side door, and light spilled out over them. "Here we go!" she said.

She boosted Annie up into the cab of the truck, then followed her. She slammed the door and the cabin light went out. Once again, Annie was surrounded by the sound of the rain and the muted light from a dashboard.

From behind, they heard clanking sounds as the man who drove the truck hooked a cable to their car. Then there was a whirring as he used a winch to drag the car back onto the road. After a few more clanks and bangs, the driver-side door opened and the biggest man Annie had ever seen climbed into the cabin.

At school, Annie's librarian had been reading stories called tall tales to her class. When Annie saw this man, she immediately thought of the giant woodsman from those stories, Paul Bunyan. The tow truck driver seemed too big to get through the door. He had curly hair and a curly brown beard. He was wearing a dark rain slicker, but underneath it Annie could see he had on a checked flannel shirt.

As he climbed into the cab, the man smiled warmly at Annie.

"Hello, little lady," he said. "How are you? A little wet?"

Annie smiled. She liked the man immediately. "Yes," she said.

"Well, we'll fix that," the man said as he closed the door behind him. He turned up the heat and directed a vent at Annie.

"Better?" he asked.

Annie nodded.

"Good," he said. "Then let's get you and your mom home."

He looked over his shoulder, then pulled out onto the road. His big truck sliced through the sheets of rain like a ship through the sea.

"Thank you so much for helping us," Annie's mom told the driver. "I don't know how long we would have been stuck there if you hadn't come by."

"My pleasure, ma'am," he said.

Annie was looking around the cab of the truck when a soft gleam of light near the rearview mirror caught her eye. She looked up and saw something hanging there.

"What's that?" she asked.

The big man looked where she was pointing, then glanced down at her.

"That," the man said, "is my good luck charm. Would you like to see it?"

Annie nodded, and the man handed it down to her. It was an angel—a cherub—made of porcelain, with golden hair and wings.

Annie thought she had never seen anything so beautiful.

"It's really something, isn't it?" the man asked.

Staring at the angel, Annie nodded.

"There's a story that goes with it," he

said. "One night, several years ago—a night very much like this one, in fact—I was stranded on the side of the road with a dead battery. A very nice lady stopped and helped me get going again. Before she left, she gave that to me. I didn't want to take it from her, but she insisted. I've had it ever since."

Annie caressed one delicate wing with her forefinger.

"It's brought me good luck all these years," the big man was saying. He paused, then looked down at Annie. "But a gift like that is meant to be passed on. What do you think? Would you like to keep it?"

Annie's heart leaped. "Oh, yes!" she said.

But Annie's mom was shaking her head. "You've done too much for us already," she said. "We can't take this from you."

The man smiled. "You're not taking it from me, I'm giving it to you. Please. I'd like your little girl to have it."

Annie's mom considered for a moment, then smiled. "All right," she said. "I don't know what to say."

"Thank you?" Annie suggested.

The man and her mother laughed.

"That's exactly right," her mom said. *"Thank you."*

Annie smiled and clutched the angel tightly to her chest. It was the best Christmas gift she'd ever received.

THREE

Lost in memory, Grandpa stopped talking. Simon and Lucy waited. Finally, Lucy said, "That's a great story, Grandpa."

"Hmm?" Grandpa said, slowly coming back to the present. "What? Oh, yes, isn't it though?"

"What about the name?" Lucy asked, showing him the bottom of the figurine.

"Ah!" Grandpa said. "Well, after Annie and her mother were delivered home safely that night, they told me the whole story. When they were through, A ie wanted to name the angel.

"Her favorite name was Mary. But she couldn't use that name, because a rather important person in the Christmas story had already claimed it."

"So instead," Simon interjected with a laugh, "she used that name for her first daughter!"

Grandpa nodded. "Right you are! But Annie also loved the name Lucy. So she and her mother looked it up in a book of names. They discovered that it comes from the Latin name Lucius, which means 'bringing light.'

"Well, the angel had certainly brought light that night. It was the perfect name. I can remember Annie sitting right there on the floor, writing the name on the bottom of the figure.

"After that, Lucy had a special place on the tree," Grandpa continued. "It wasn't until your mother went away to college that Lucy disappeared."

Grandpa smiled at the real Lucy. "But I always liked to think we had found our little angel again, in you."

Lucy smiled. She stood up and gave her grandfather a kiss. "Thanks, Grandpa. It's a wonderful story."

"You're welcome, honey," he said.

Simon shook his head. "It's kind of amazing. That little figurine has seen a lot."

They all looked at the porcelain angel for a moment. Then Lucy said, "Grandpa, would it be okay with you if we took the angel home to Mom tomorrow? I can just picture her face when we give it to her."

"That's a wonderful idea," Grandpa said. "I can't think of a better Christmas gift."

The next morning, Lucy woke with a smile on her face. She had a feeling it was going to be a fabulous day. Not only was it Christmas Eve, not only was she going to sing at the party tonight, but she also had something special to give to her mother.

On her way to the shower, Lucy poked her head into Simon's room. The alarm next to his bed was beeping away, but Simon was doing a good job of ignoring it. He was sprawled facedown on the bed, hiding underneath the covers.

"Simon . . . ," Lucy said gently. "Little brother . . . time to get up . . ."

Simon was doing a good job of ignoring her, too.

Lucy sighed. "Simon," she said louder. "Simon!"

"Wha—" Simon gasped, jerking his head up. Blankets askew, he turned and squinted in the general direction of the doorway. When he saw Lucy standing there, he groaned and dropped his head back to the pillow.

"Oh, no you don't," Lucy said. "It's a six-hour drive home, and I don't want to be late for the party. *Get up.*"

Simon didn't move.

Time to play dirty, Lucy thought. As casually as she could, she said, "I'd think *you'd* want to be there early, too. Isn't what's-her-name supposed to be there?"

Without lifting his head, Simon said, "Her name's Ashley. And I have no idea if she's going to be there."

"Well," Lucy said. "If she *does* come, you wouldn't want to keep her waiting. Not with all that mistletoe—and all those eligible young men hanging around . . ."

Simon growled and whipped his pillow at the doorway, but Lucy was already gone, sailing down the hall to the bathroom.

Mission accomplished, she thought happily. *Christmas party, here I come!*

Several hours later, Lucy's good mood had disappeared. She'd wanted to be on the road by eleven o'clock. Thanks to Simon, it was almost one before they were ready to go.

"Who takes hour-long showers?" Lucy asked as they carried their bags downstairs.

"*I* do," Simon retorted. "Especially when somebody gets me up too early!"

"Oh, great," Lucy said. "So it's *my* fault you're inconsiderate."

"Oh, come on," Simon said. "What's the big deal? It's a six-hour drive at the most. The party isn't until eight. We've got plenty of time."

"You call an extra hour plenty of time?" Lucy asked. She shook her head. "You'd better hope nothing bad happens on the way home."

"Ooh," Simon said. "You mean we might get a flat tire? Or maybe we'll get carjacked."

"Don't joke," Lucy said. "You never know what could happen."

Simon rolled his eyes, but before he could say anything, they were walking into the kitchen. Grandpa and Ginger were waiting for them. Immediately, they were all smiles.

"It's been so nice having you here!" Ginger said.

"I hope you can come again soon," Grandpa said. "Do you have Lucy?"

Lucy smiled. "Of course," she said, patting her bag. "I'm going to hang her on the rearview mirror for the drive home."

"Excellent idea," Grandpa said.

"Now, you've got the cell phone, right?" Ginger asked as they walked to the door.

"Check," said Simon.

"And plenty of money?" asked Grandpa.

"Check, check," Simon said.

"Call us right away if you have any problems, okay?" Ginger said.

"Okay," Lucy said, "but I'm sure we'll be fine."

Simon raised an eyebrow, but said nothing.

"I am, too," said Ginger. She gave each of them a hug. "Drive safely, and take your time."

"We will," said Lucy. She and Simon hugged their grandfather, then started for the car. Simon and Lucy's parents had loaned them the family minivan for the drive to Grandpa and Ginger's.

"Hey," Simon said. "I haven't had a chance to drive yet. What do you say? Care to put yourself in my hands on the way home?"

"Ha!" Lucy said. "You expect me to let you drive after you've made us late? No way."

Simon looked at Lucy in surprise. "Huh? Come on! Mom and Dad said I could!"

Lucy took the angel out of her bag, then threw her bag in the back. "Forget it," she said. "You're not responsible enough to get up on time, you're not responsible enough to drive."

"I can't believe you," Simon said. He flung his bag into the back with Lucy's, then climbed into the passenger seat. "I'm not a little kid anymore!"

"Sometimes you act like one," Lucy said, sliding in behind the wheel and hanging the angel on the rearview mirror.

Simon shook his head in disbelief.

"And sometimes you can be such a jerk," he said. He crossed his arms and looked out his window.

Lucy started the car and fastened her seat belt. She waved to Grandpa and Ginger, then put the minivan in reverse and carefully backed out of the driveway.

They weren't even out of the neighborhood before Simon's arms had relaxed and his head was lolling against the window.

He's asleep! Lucy thought incredulously. *And slacking on his duties again.* Since he was in the passenger seat, Simon was supposed to watch the map and keep an eye out for road signs.

Lucy opened her mouth to wake him, then closed it again. She needed some peace and quiet anyway. She turned the radio on low and settled back into her seat.

When the entrance to the interstate came up, Lucy decided not to take it. Instead, she stayed on the state road. It was a two-laner with little traffic. Occasionally, it passed through small towns, but by and large, they'd be driving through the country.

Lucy smiled. That sort of drive—quiet,

peaceful—was just what she needed right now.

Besides, Lucy wasn't very comfortable on the interstate: too many cars going way too fast. And although she'd never admit it, Simon was right. They had plenty of time to get home. Unless, of course, something unforeseen happened.

But Simon was probably right about that, too. What could possibly happen?

FOUR

The next couple of hours passed uneventfully. At one point, Simon woke up. He groggily looked over at his sister, scowled, and went back to sleep.

Lucy sighed. *I ought to apologize,* she thought. *I really <u>was</u> a jerk. I was nervous about getting on the road, and I took it out on him.*

Lucy promised herself that when Simon finally woke up, she'd let him know she was sorry.

Thirty minutes later, she forgot all about her promise. She was peering worriedly at the sky. It was getting dark, and the wind was picking up.

Nothing to worry about, she told herself

nervously. *So maybe it's going to rain. A little rain never hurt anything.*

Still, Lucy was concerned. She and Grandpa had watched the weather report the night before, and there hadn't been any mention of rain or winds.

Beside her, Simon stirred again. He was awake, but he didn't look at her. Or talk to her. Lucy glanced over. He just shifted and stared out his window.

Still mad at me, she thought.

"Simon—" she began.

"I'm hungry," he said abruptly. "And I need to use the bathroom."

Lucy sighed. "Sure," she said. "Do you want to stop at the next gas station? We could use some gas anyway."

Simon turned toward Lucy. "Are you asking for my opinion? I thought *kids* didn't get any say in *adult* decisions."

For a moment, Lucy felt her temper rise. But then she remembered she was trying to make up with her brother.

"Simon—" she began again.

"Save it," Simon said, turning back to his window.

Lucy sighed again. *I understand why he's angry,* she thought. *Still, he knows I'm trying to apologize, and he's being a jerk about it.*

Lucy gripped the wheel a little harder, and she and Simon rode on in silence.

Not long after, they drove into a small town. At one of its two stoplights, there was a gas station with a minimart. Lucy pulled in. She'd barely brought the car to a stop at the pump before Simon was opening his door and heading for the store.

"Get me some chips!" she called.

Simon pretended he hadn't heard her.

Lucy shook her head. *He'd better get me some chips,* she thought. She got out of the car and started filling the tank. The clouds were getting lower and darker, and the wind was picking up. As it gusted through the gas station, it lifted her hair and whipped it across her face.

Lucy was definitely getting nervous. *Calm down,* she told herself. *Even if it rains so hard that we have to pull over, we've got time.*

There was *no way* she was missing that party.

As Lucy returned the gas nozzle to the pump, she saw a pregnant woman on the other side of the lot walking back and forth next to a brown sedan.

The woman saw Lucy looking at her. She smiled and waved. Lucy smiled and waved back. Then she closed the minivan's gas tank with a snap and headed into the minimart.

Inside, Simon was paying for a bunch of food. Lucy noticed that he *had* picked up a bag of chips. She smiled.

"Thanks," she said as she came up next to him.

"For what?" he said.

Lucy gestured at the chips.

"Oh," said Simon. He shrugged. "I wanted some, too."

Great, Lucy thought. She asked the cashier to include the price of the gas with the food and got out her wallet.

"You kids going far?" the man asked them as he rang up their purchases.

"We're heading home to Glenoak, a town outside of LA," Lucy said. "We've been visiting our grandparents in Phoenix."

The man glanced out the store window. Lucy looked, too, and was shocked to see that it was even darker outside than when she'd come in the store just a minute ago!

The man shook his head. "So you're right smack in the middle, no closer to one than the other."

Lucy nodded.

"Because if it made any sense, which it doesn't, I'd say you should turn around and go back to your grandparents'."

Simon spoke up. "Why do you say that?" he asked.

The man gestured to a portable radio sitting next to the cash register. "I've been listening to that all morning," he said. "This storm's surprised everybody, and it's turning out to be a big one. They're recommending that everyone stay indoors. In fact, I'm shutting down the store and heading home myself. You two are my last customers."

Stay calm, Lucy thought. To the man she said, "How bad could it be? Rain, wind—"

"Hail, lightning, flooding," the man said. "These desert storms can get really bad."

Lucy's face must have turned white, because suddenly the man smiled and said, "Hey, I didn't mean to scare you. Don't worry, you'll be fine. If worse comes to worst, just pull over to the side of the road, turn on your flashers, and wait it out. You'll be perfectly safe in your car."

Lucy paid the guy, and Simon took the bag of food. "Thanks," she said.

The man nodded. "Be careful," he replied.

Simon and Lucy headed outside into the whistling wind. They pushed through it to the car. As Lucy climbed into the driver's seat, she looked across the lot and saw that the pregnant woman was still there, standing next to her car. The woman was watching Lucy; she waved and smiled again.

Lucy turned to Simon. "That woman is alone. I'm going to go ask her if she needs any help. Would you do me a favor and call Grandpa and Ginger on the cell? I want to know what they think we should do."

"Sure," Simon said, taking the cell phone out of his pocket.

"Thanks," Lucy said. She got out of the car, shut her door, and trudged through the wind to the woman across the lot.

The woman smiled as Lucy walked up. "Some weather we're having, huh?" she said over the wind.

"Are you okay?" Lucy asked. "Do you need any help?"

The woman shook her head. "I'm fine. My car just quit," she said. She gestured to the pay phone next to her car. "I called a tow truck. Should be here any time."

Up close, the woman looked *very* pregnant, as if she were expecting pretty soon.

The woman must have noticed Lucy noticing, because she put a hand on her stomach. "Don't worry," she said. "You're nice to be concerned, but I've got over a week to go. Now you go ahead and get back in your car. Your parents must be worried sick!"

Lucy smiled. "Yeah," she said. "Well, take care."

"You too, sweetheart. Drive safely," the woman said.

Lucy hurried back to the minivan and climbed behind the wheel.

"What did Grandpa and Ginger say?" she asked as she slammed the door, shutting out the wind.

"The phone isn't working," Simon said. "It must be the storm."

He gestured toward the woman across the lot. "What's her story?" he asked.

"Car trouble," Lucy said, starting up the minivan. "She's called a tow truck, but I don't know. . . . She's pregnant."

"What do you want to do?" Simon asked.

"I don't know," Lucy said. She looked at the woman, then up at the sky. "I guess we'd better go. There's no telling how long we'll have to stop once this storm hits."

Lucy pulled out of the gas station. On the road, they could both feel how much stronger the wind had become. It pushed at the minivan. Lucy gripped the wheel and thought of the woman standing in this wind, waiting for a tow truck.

I hope she's gotten in the car, Lucy thought. She glanced in the rearview mirror, as if she might be able to catch a glimpse of the woman and her car, but the gas station had already disappeared around a bend in the road.

Lucy's eyes dropped to the angel figurine swinging beneath the mirror. In the growing darkness, the flawless porcelain looked as if it were glowing. The angel's gilded wings and hair almost gave off a soft light.

Bringer of light, Lucy thought. She

looked down the road. It seemed to roll on without end. And the sky was close to black.

Lucy glanced in the rearview mirror to be sure there was no one behind them, then pulled over and stopped the car. She looked at Simon.

"I don't feel right about leaving her out there," she said.

Simon looked back at her. She thought he looked a little relieved. "I don't, either," he said.

"You realize we might miss the party," Lucy said.

Simon shrugged. "I never liked what's-her-name all that much anyway."

Lucy laughed. She turned the car around and headed back to the gas station.

FIVE

When they pulled into the lot, the woman's brown sedan was still there, but the woman was nowhere in sight.

Good, Lucy thought, hoping she'd taken shelter in the minimart. But the store was dark. The cashier had already locked up and left.

They pulled up and parked beside the woman's sedan. There didn't seem to be anyone in the car.

Simon looked at Lucy. "Maybe she got a ride with the tow truck driver?" he suggested.

"But why wouldn't they take the car?" Lucy said. "Come on, let's take a look."

They got out and walked over to the

sedan. Several feet from the door, they had their answer. The woman was in the car after all, lying down across the front seat.

Lucy and Simon hurried to her door, and Lucy knocked on the window.

The woman looked up. When she saw who it was, she smiled. She sat up and rolled down her window.

"What are you kids doing back here?" she asked. "I thought I told you to get home!"

"You did," Lucy said, returning the woman's smile, "but I was worried about you. Are you sure you're okay?"

"Maybe we can take you somewhere," Simon interjected. "Get you out of this storm."

The woman smiled again. "You two are really sweet," she said, "but that tow truck should be here any minute now, and—"

The woman broke off. Her eyes closed, and her face tightened in pain.

"What is it?" Simon asked. "What's wrong?"

After a moment, the woman let out a breath and collapsed back onto the seat. "Oh, Lord," she said. "Why now?"

Suddenly Lucy knew. "You just had a

contraction!" she said. "Didn't you?"

The woman paused, then nodded wearily. "But that doesn't change anything," she said. "That tow truck driver . . ."

"He's not coming," Lucy said, suddenly sure of it. In her mind, she could see the tow truck driver from Grandpa's story of the night before. The night he'd rescued her mother and grandmother, he'd carried the angel. Today, it was she and Simon who were bringing the light.

"Simon and I are here," Lucy went on. "We'd like to help, if you'll let us."

The woman looked at Lucy for a moment, then nodded. "All right," she said.

Simon opened her door and helped her out. As they climbed into the minivan, the woman laughed.

"I was praying for someone to come," she said. "But I never thought I'd look up and see you two angels in my window!"

When they'd settled the woman across the backseat, Lucy motioned to Simon. They moved to the front of the minivan.

"You still want to drive?" Lucy asked quietly.

Simon looked stunned. "Well, yeah, but . . ." He gestured to the windshield. As if to make his point, fat raindrops began smacking against the glass, slowly at first, and then faster. ". . . in this weather?" he finished.

"One of us has to stay with her," Lucy said. "I think that should be me. That means *you've* got to drive."

Simon took a deep breath. He looked back at the woman lying across the back-seat. The rain was beginning to come down harder now. The rapping on the roof of the minivan was turning into a steady roar.

"Okay," Simon said. "I'll try."

"You can do it," Lucy said. "Just take it slow."

Simon nodded. "Okay." He climbed into the driver's seat, and Lucy went back to sit with the woman.

"Is he going to be okay?" the woman asked, a smile on her lips. "He looks about as scared as I feel!"

Lucy laughed. "He's going to be great," she said. "He's just never driven in weather like this."

"Have you?" the woman asked.

"Ah . . . no," Lucy admitted.

"That makes three of us," she said.

They laughed as Simon backed the van up, then pulled out of the lot and onto the road.

"Where am I going?" he called back.

"There's a hospital—" The woman broke off. Her body stiffened, and she grabbed Lucy's hand and squeezed.

Lucy squeezed back.

When the contraction had passed, she took a breath and said, ". . . in Barkley. Just follow this road, go through the next town, and it's the town after that."

"Got that, Simon?" Lucy called.

"Got it," Simon said.

Lucy turned back to the woman. "What can I do?" she asked.

"Nothing, I'm afraid," the woman said. She smiled. "Except talk to me a little. What's your name?"

"Lucy. And this is my brother Simon."

"Hello!" Simon called over his shoulder.

"I'm very glad to meet you both," the woman said. "My name is Meredith."

"Hello, Meredith," Lucy said.

Meredith smiled. "Why don't you tell me about your family, Lucy? What are you and Simon doing out on this rainy Christmas Eve?"

So Lucy told Meredith about visiting their grandfather in Phoenix and about the rest of their family in Glenoak. As she talked, Meredith listened quietly, occasionally closing her eyes and squeezing Lucy's hand.

When Lucy noticed sweat starting to dampen the hair on Meredith's forehead, she found a napkin in the now-forgotten bag of food and mopped her brow.

Simon was driving slowly but steadily. Although Meredith's contractions were becoming more frequent, Lucy felt confident they'd get to the hospital in time.

Then the car slowed and came to a stop.

Meredith was in the middle of a contraction and didn't notice. Lucy moved to the front of the minivan.

Simon was sitting with his arms at his sides, staring out the windshield. He looked defeated.

"What's wrong?" Lucy said quietly. "Simon! Why'd you stop the car?"

He looked at Lucy helplessly. "I can't

see," he said. "How am I supposed to drive if I can't see?"

Lucy's gaze lifted to the windshield, and she felt her heart drop. Simon was right. The rain was coming down so hard, the windshield was nothing but a blurry sheet of water. All Lucy could see was gray light and vague shapes.

Beside her, Simon was shaking his head. "What are we going to do?" he said. "What are we going to do?"

SIX

Think, Lucy reasoned. *Think!*

Simon was getting upset. Even though she thought she felt as panicked as he did, someone had to keep it together.

Lucy put her hand on Simon's shoulder. "We'll wait it out," she said. "What else can we do?"

Simon nodded. "Okay," he said. "How's Meredith? Is she okay?"

"She's doing all right," Lucy lied. For the last five or ten minutes, Meredith's contractions had been getting worse, and they'd been coming closer and closer together. But she wasn't going to tell Simon that.

"If it starts to let up—" Lucy began.

"I know," Simon said. "I will."

Lucy went back to Meredith. The woman was panting and groaning. Her face was covered with sweat. Lucy reached for a fresh napkin, but she'd used them all.

"What's wrong?" Meredith said.

"What do you mean?" asked Lucy, leaning toward Meredith's side.

Meredith opened her eyes a crack and smiled as best she could. "Honey, don't kid a kidder," she said. "I can hear you two up there whispering. What's going on?"

Lucy sighed. "We're stopped," she said. "The rain's coming down too hard for Simon to see."

Meredith closed her eyes. "Oh, Lord," she said. She cried out as another convulsion wracked her body.

Lucy felt like crying. It was so frustrating. What could she do? Suddenly she thought of Grandpa, waiting by the phone thirty-five years ago for word from his wife and child, unable to do anything but . . .

"Sing," Lucy said aloud.

Meredith hadn't heard her. She was deep inside herself with the pain of giving birth.

Lucy closed her eyes. Overhead, the rain striking the roof of the minivan was a constant thunder. In the front of the car, Simon sat silently, staring out the windshield, waiting for the rain to let up. Lucy could almost hear his worry. Meredith lay on the seat, struggling.

Lucy lifted her head and took a breath. Without consciously making the decision, she found herself singing one of the carols she would have sung at the church party, which suddenly seemed a world away.

"O holy night, the stars are brightly shining. . . ."

She sang quietly, but her sweet voice slipped past the roar of the rain to find her brother in the front of the van and Meredith in the back.

Lucy sang the carol through. When she had finished, she opened her eyes. Meredith was gazing at her. Her eyes were clear, and her face was shining.

"You're an angel," Meredith said quietly. She smiled. "You sing like an angel."

Lucy grinned. "Thank you," she said. "How are you feeling?"

"I feel blessed," Meredith said.

"Hey!" Simon shouted from up front. "I can see! I can see!"

Lucy heard him put the car in gear, and they started to move.

Meredith's face pinched as another contraction started. "Don't stop," she gasped. "Please."

Lucy sang through all the carols she would have sung with the choir that night, and then some, before they found the hospital and Meredith was whisked away.

Simon parked the car, and he and Lucy dragged themselves inside to wait.

They collapsed in chairs in the waiting room. Across the room, a TV hung from the ceiling.

"I guess we should make some phone calls," Lucy said. "People are going to be worried."

Simon nodded, then turned to look at his sister. "We did it," he said. "We did it!"

Lucy could see that he was tired, but his eyes were bright. She smiled.

"You did a great job," she said. "Driving through that weather wasn't easy."

"Yeah," Simon said. He shook his head. "It was terrifying, especially knowing that Meredith was depending on me."

They sat for a while and stared at nothing, listening to the babble of voices from the TV. The waiting room was almost empty. There were red and green streamers hung on the wall. Above the nurse's station was a HAPPY HOLIDAYS! sign.

Lucy finally roused herself, and she and Simon made their calls, first to Grandpa and Ginger and then to their parents. They explained what had happened and that they wouldn't be back in time for the party. They wanted to wait around until Meredith had her baby.

"Of course!" their mom said.

"I'd expect nothing less," said their father on the extension. "And if you're out too late, use the credit card to get a hotel room. You shouldn't be driving if you're tired."

"And Mom . . . ," Lucy said. She wanted to tell her about the angel.

"What is it?" her mom asked.

"Nothing," Lucy finally said. "We'll see you at home."

"Okay, kids," said Reverend Camden. "Drive safely."

They hung up. Simon was looking at Lucy quizzically.

"Why didn't you tell her about the angel?" he asked.

"Because I'm not sure we'll still have it," Lucy said.

"Huh?" Simon asked.

"I have an idea, but you need to agree to it," said Lucy. "It seems the right thing to do. . . ."

Later that night, a nurse ushered them into Meredith's room. She'd had her baby—a healthy little boy!

The nurse left them. Meredith lay in bed under a white sheet. Her eyes were closed. The baby had been wrapped in a blanket and tucked in the crook of her arm.

"Meredith?" Lucy said softly. If she was sleeping, Lucy didn't want to wake her.

Meredith's eyes fluttered open, and she smiled.

"Simon, Lucy!" she said. "I'm glad to see you."

Lucy and Simon came to the side of the bed and peered down at Meredith's child.

Lucy gasped. "He's so precious!" she said.

Meredith laughed. "Yes, he is, isn't he?"

Simon just shook his head. "Wow," he said.

Lucy stole a glance at Meredith. Her face was positively glowing!

Meredith looked up and caught Lucy's eye. "There is no way I can ever thank you enough," she said, "for what you did tonight. You may well have saved my life, and the life of this child."

Lucy shook her head. "We only did what was right."

Meredith smiled. "How proud your parents must be, to have such confident, capable children. My husband is grateful to you, too. His plane was delayed due to the storm, but he's on his way here now."

For a while, the three were silent, looking down at Meredith's child as he slept. Then Lucy said, "We have to go. But first, we wanted to give you something."

Simon had gone back to the car and was carrying the food bag from the minimart. From it, he lifted the angel.

Meredith gasped. "It's beautiful!" she said.

"It's our gift to your child," Lucy said. "If you'll have it."

Simon handed the angel to Meredith. She took it and examined its gilded wings and hair. Then she shook her head.

"How can I accept a gift from you, when you've already given me so much today?"

"Please," Lucy insisted. "We want you to have it."

Meredith looked down at her baby, then back at the angel. "All right," she said. She smiled. "Thank you."

Simon spoke up. "And there's a story that goes with it, too." And he told her about the man who had helped their mother when she was a child, and about the woman who had helped him.

"And you, in turn, helped me," Meredith said. She looked down at her child again. "Are you sure you don't want to take it home to your mother?" she asked.

Lucy shook her head. "This is the right thing to do. But there is one thing. When your baby's old enough, he might want to give the angel a name. Unfortunately, my mom did, too."

Lucy reached forward to show Meredith the name written on the bottom of the angel. But when she turned it over . . .

Lucy and Simon gasped. The name was gone! The porcelain was as bright as the day it had been made.

Meredith took the angel back from Lucy and put it on her bedside table. "And now," she said, "it's time for you kids to get home to spend Christmas Eve with your family."

Lucy looked at Simon in wonder. Simon just smiled and shrugged.

Lucy looked back at Meredith, lying with her child in the crook of her arm, her face glowing.

"Yes," Lucy said. "It is."

SEVEN

On the way out to the car, Lucy finally apologized to Simon for her behavior earlier that day.

"I was just nervous about the long drive, and I took it out on you," Lucy said. "I'm really sorry."

"Wow," Simon said. "Can I get this on tape? I want to play it back again and again and again. . . ."

Simon laughed as Lucy pushed him playfully.

"That is officially the last time I ever apologize to you," she said.

When he got to the car, Lucy asked him if he wanted to drive.

"Are you kidding?" he said. "I'm not

sure I'll ever want to drive again!"

Lucy smiled as she unlocked the car and climbed in. "Somehow, I think you will."

The rest of the drive home was as uneventful as Lucy had hoped the entire trip would be. The sky had cleared and the rain had stopped, but Lucy drove slowly anyway. It was dark, and the stars burned clearly in the sky.

It was very late when they finally pulled into their driveway in Glenoak. The house was dark.

"Is everybody asleep already?" Simon asked.

"I guess so," Lucy said. She felt a little disappointed. She'd been looking forward to seeing everyone. "I can't believe it's Christmas Eve."

"It isn't," Simon said, checking his watch. "It's officially Christmas now."

They trudged up the walk and went in the front door. Lucy was reaching for the light switch when Simon said, "Wait."

"What?" Lucy asked.

Simon pointed. Lucy could see soft red and green light spilling in from the . . .

"Family room?" Lucy asked.

Simon nodded. They put down their bags and followed the light. As they got closer, they could hear voices and quiet laughter.

They turned the corner into the family room. There, sitting on the couch and the floor, was the family. The regular lights were off. In the corner, the Christmas tree glowed with colored light.

"Hey!" Matt said. "Look who's finally home!"

"Well it's about time!" said Ruthie. "I've been ready to open a present for hours!"

Everyone laughed as they gathered around Simon and Lucy, hugging them and wishing them a merry Christmas.

"How was the party?" Simon asked.

Ruthie grinned. "Great," she said. "The best part was watching a certain Ashley kissing every boy in sight!"

Simon turned red. He was about to say something when his mother spoke up. "We sure did miss your singing, Lucy," she said.

"Oh, Mom," Lucy said. "Simon and I found something special for you." She told her the whole story of the angel—how they'd found it in the attic, how Grandpa had told them its story, and how they'd decided to pass it on to Meredith.

When Lucy had finished, her mother had tears in her eyes. "I'm glad you found her after all these years," she said. "I always wondered what happened to her. I guess I always assumed she'd found another family somehow. And now she has. I'm glad you passed her on. It was the right thing to do."

Suddenly Simon spoke up. "Hey!" he said. "Where's Mary?"

There was a collective groan. The Reverend and Mrs. Camden looked at each other. "Mary won't be arriving tonight," Reverend Camden said.

"Where is she?" Simon asked.

"Last we heard—stuck in the Chicago airport under a pile of snow. . . ."

MARY'S GIFT

ONE

Mary Camden had a good reason to be upset.

It was Christmas Eve and, unlike the rest of her family, she wasn't in Glenoak. Nor was she curled up in a warm bed, or roasting chestnuts on an open fire. Mary was stranded in the Chicago airport. Alone. Waiting in an endless line of angry travelers. Just her luck.

She took a deep breath and looked out the giant windows of the airline terminal. When her flight from Buffalo had landed, the snow was light, but now a massive blizzard swirled so thick that even the blinking red lights of the runway had been erased from view. All flights were now canceled—

including her connecting flight to Los Angeles. Was there any way to get home on a night like this?

She turned to a frustrated man behind her, whose tie had been loosened and retightened so many times it looked like a dirty, crinkled napkin.

"Don't these planes have computers that control their landings?" Mary asked. "Do they really need to see the runway?"

The man guffawed. "Computers? Who needs computers? If they had real fighter pilots instead of these wimpy civilians in their flimsy corporate uniforms, we'd be home by now."

Mary laughed at the man's feisty attitude, then looked at her watch. Her eyes widened. She'd been standing in line for an hour! And not a single airline employee had offered a solution or an apology.

The man grabbed his tie and wiped a streak of doughnut jelly from his chin. "What these people deserve is a good lawsuit," he barked, loud enough for the attendant to hear. But the attendant was preoccupied with a screaming woman in a fur coat.

Mary sighed, then tried to calm herself

down. Maybe she was overreacting. Maybe the situation really was out of the airline's control . . . but she couldn't deny her irritation. There weren't even enough chairs in the lobby for half the people who'd been stranded there.

The man seemed to be reading her thoughts. "All these people are driving me crazy. Too many of them in too small a space."

Mary's eyes combed the terminal. "There's barely room to stand, let alone to sit. . . ."

The man snorted. "Well, we aren't leaving for a long time. Might as well get comfortable on the cold, dingy floor." He picked up his briefcase. "In fact, I think that's exactly what I'm going to do." And with that, he left the line.

But Mary wasn't giving up so easily. She crossed her arms and considered her options. She could continue to stand in line, knowing it would take hours to accomplish anything, or she could act. *There's no way I'm going to miss Christmas with my family. If there's a plane leaving Chicago tonight, I'm going to be on it!* she thought.

She picked up her bag and charged straight through the line of people.

"Hey, no cutting," a man yelled.

Mary ignored him and stormed up to the check-in desk, where the fur-coated woman was flailing her hands in anger.

"Excuse me," Mary began.

The woman took a giant step back and swept her arms out as though welcoming a queen. But her eyes were far from respectful. "No, excuse me!" she shouted, displeased by the interruption. Her fingers were covered in tacky, oversize diamonds.

But Mary was undeterred. She propped her elbows on the desk and leaned over to the attendant. "If I were the President of the United States, and I demanded to be put on a flight tonight— would you put me on it?"

The attendant, not amused, calmly remarked, "Seeing as your life would be the most important of any in the entire nation, no, I'd prefer to preserve it."

The haughty woman tried to look down her nose at Mary, then realized that Mary was taller than she thought. She looked up her nose instead.

"I'm the wife of the Governor of California. Do you really think this man would put you on a plane before taking care of me?"

Mary ignored the tone of the woman's voice, although she couldn't deny the sinking feeling in the pit of her stomach: if this wealthy, important woman couldn't get on a flight tonight, how could Mary?

Mary looked at the attendant.

"Then can you put me in a hotel?"

"They're all full," the Governor's wife cooed, savoring Mary's reaction. Then she pulled out a cell phone and began dialing a number. "Luckily, there's a suite reserved for me, regardless of what city I'm in."

Mary shot the woman a venomous look and turned to go. She'd find a hotel room if it was the last thing she did.

Thirty minutes later, Mary had called every hotel in the Yellow Pages except one. She looked down at the ten numbers that symbolized her last hope, then crossed her fingers and dialed. A male clerk picked up the line.

"Sorry, no vac—"

Mary raced to get her words out.

"Don't hang up until you've heard me out! Do you have any rooms?"

The clerk cut in. "Sorry—"

"Even an empty office or a janitor's closet?"

"No vacancy."

The line went dead and Mary stood staring at the phone in her hand. *Unbelievable. There are no rooms in the entire city of Chicago.*

Suddenly Mary couldn't help but laugh at the irony of her name. Poor little Mary can't find a room at an inn on Christmas Eve! But the laugh quickly turned into a grimace: the name Mary was about the only thing she had in common with her biblical namesake. The biblical Mary was the Mother of God, but Mary Camden . . . what had she ever accomplished besides jail time and a family ousting? The last good thing she had done was win a stupid basketball game—and then trash the gym she won it in.

Suddenly Mary felt really low. She picked up the phone and dialed, hoping Robbie would answer and make her feel better.

The familiar voice of Mary's on-again,

off-again boyfriend came through the line. "Hello?"

Mary felt tears welling up in her eyes. "I'm stuck in the stupid Chicago airport. I won't be home for Christmas Eve."

There was a short pause. "Well, you'll be home tomorrow, right? You'll be home for Christmas?"

Mary looked out the window, where the blizzard was raging even fiercer than before. "I don't know. . . ."

There was another pause, and then Robbie did the dumbest thing he could have done: he laughed. "Hey, the twins are sick anyway. Maybe we'll get their stomach flu and you'll be the lucky one who misses out."

Mary couldn't believe he was making light of the situation. "Lucky? You call this lucky!"

"I didn't say you were lucky. I said maybe you'll be the lucky one who misses out on their flu. I was trying to make a joke."

"Well, it's not funny, Robbie! I'm stuck in this stupid place, with stupid strangers, with no beds and no blankets and no showers on Christmas Eve!"

"I'm sorry, I wanted to make you laugh."

Mary wiped away a tear. Lately, it felt like Robbie didn't care about seeing her nearly as much as she cared about seeing him. "You don't even care if I get home, do you?"

Robbie sighed. "I was trying to make you feel better, Mary. And it didn't work. So maybe what you need to do is just accept the situation. That's the only thing that will make the night bearable."

That's when Mary felt a tug on her coat. She turned around to find a six- or seven-year-old girl with fire-red hair staring up at her. Her blinking green eyes seemed the size of quarters.

"Where's the bathroom?" the little girl asked.

Mary covered the mouthpiece of the phone and leaned down. "You see that blue sign way down there, across the hall?"

The little girl smiled and darted off.

"Hey!" Mary called. "Wait!"

But it was too late. The little girl was already lost in the crowd.

Robbie continued to talk, but Mary found herself missing every other word.

That little girl . . . why was she asking *Mary* about the bathroom? Where were her parents? Her guardians? Who would leave a kid alone in an airport?

"Sorry, Robbie, I gotta go!" Mary exclaimed.

"Why? Are you mad?"

"I'll call you later!"

She hung up the phone and dashed off after the little girl.

TWO

Just before Mary reached the bathroom entrance, she ran head-on into a stranger. His bags went flying, and Mary's foot, caught in a trailing shoulder strap, flew out from under her. She tumbled sideways and landed gracelessly on the floor. "Ouch!"

The stranger dropped to his knees and held out his hand. "I'm so sorry. Are you okay?"

Mary laughed. "I knew this night could only get worse!" But then she looked at the young man and realized that maybe her night had gotten better. She was staring straight into the eyes of a Justin Timberlake look-alike. He even had the curly blond hair and long, lanky body.

She smiled and took his hand.

"I'm Clayton," he said as he lifted her up.

She shook her head. "That was my fault. I've always been a klutz."

Clayton grinned. "I'm the one carrying seven bags. I'm a walking obstacle course."

Mary's brow furrowed as she took note of all his luggage. "Why do you have so many bags?"

"It's easier than going to the gym."

Mary laughed. "Okay . . ."

Clayton shook his curly head, indicating that he was joking. "I'm here with a group of kids. I'm helping out with the bags."

The word *kid* suddenly reminded Mary of her mission. She thanked Clayton for helping her up, then started to go. "I hate to hit and run, but I have to find somebody. . . ."

He smiled and two dimples appeared in his cheeks. "Oh, sure, walk into my life and walk right back out again."

Mary laughed. "Maybe we'll bump into each other again before this dreadful night is over."

Clayton smiled as she walked away. "If

I don't see you, merry Christmas."

She looked over her shoulder. "Yeah, you too. Merry Christmas."

Clayton watched the last strand of her long hair disappear into the bathroom. Then he turned around to a group of kids standing behind him. They all wore matching shirts that said CENTRAL VALLEY YOUTH GROUP. They started whistling and laughing at their leader. "Clayton has a crush!"

Mary entered the bathroom and looked around in amazement. It was more crowded than the terminal, and almost as large. There were two wings, separated by a wall, and countless stalls in each wing. How could she ever find the little girl in this place?

She surveyed the line of people, hoping that she would be there. After all, only a few minutes had passed since she'd tugged at Mary's coat.

Mary's eyes settled on the back of a redheaded child who stood in the front of the line. Mary started toward the girl, but just as she was about to reach out and tap her shoulder, the bathroom attendant cleared her throat.

"No cutting, please."

Mary turned around and smiled. "I'm not. I'm looking for someone."

Just then, the little girl turned around and Mary saw that her eyes were brown. Not only that, the girl was holding a woman's hand. Definitely the wrong kid.

Maybe I should look under the stalls for her little feet.

Mary walked to the first stall and peeked down under the door. An old lady's worn-out loafers stared back. Mary moved to the next stall, bent over, and spotted a pair of gigantic galoshes. Nope.

She moved down the stalls until she finally spied a little girl's pair of two-toned green-and-white shoes.

She smiled. The girl had been wearing green! She knew that it was her. But what should she do next? Knock? Or wait until the girl came out?

Mary felt a tap on her shoulder. She turned to see the bathroom attendant staring at her.

"Who are you looking for, miss?"

Before Mary had time to think, the lie came out. "My little sister."

The attendant's mouth tightened as

though she knew Mary was lying. "What's her name?"

Mary swallowed. "Hillary."

The woman leaned over and knocked on the door. "Hillary? Is that you in there?"

There was no answer.

The woman narrowed her eyes at Mary. "What's your name?"

"Mary."

The woman nodded, then called out loudly, her voice resonating throughout the entire bathroom. "Hillary? Mary's looking for you. Are you here, Hillary?"

The whole bathroom fell silent as the travelers all waited for a response. There was none. The woman tried again.

"Hillary, if you're here, please respond. Mary is looking for you."

Nothing.

The woman shrugged and shooed Mary out. "Sorry."

Mary hesitated at the exit, but the woman was right on her heels, arms crossed. Mary sighed and rolled her eyes.

"Jeez, I'm going."

She pretended to walk away, joining up with a crowd of people heading down the terminal hallway. But after a few seconds, she turned to make sure the woman had gone back into the bathroom. She had.

Mary walked back to the bathroom entrance and planted herself across from it. She was going to wait for the little girl to come out, and then find out why she was alone. Maybe she'd been abandoned? Or maybe her parents were looking for her?

Just then, the bathroom attendant walked back out. She looked straight at Mary, as though she had expected her to return. She frowned. "Listen, lady, we get a lot of weirdos in this place, and I hope you're not one of them. Why don't you mosey on back to your terminal before I have to call security?"

Mary's jaw dropped. *Security? This woman actually thinks I want to kidnap a child!*

Mary sighed. She was at a loss. Not knowing what else to do, she gave up and walked away.

THREE

Defeated, Mary returned to her gate and spotted an empty strip of floor. It was uncarpeted, but at least it looked fairly clean. She started toward it, then noticed the Governor's wife sprawled out on a chair. So she hadn't gotten a hotel room after all. Mary felt a catty twinge of satisfaction, then brushed it away, determined to think more positive thoughts. *Maybe there's a reason for me to be here. . . .*

Mary reached the empty space and sat down. She looked around her, amazed that people were so desperate for sleep that they were even curled up on tables. It wasn't an exciting prospect: sleeping knee to knee with strangers on hard, cold floors. But weariness was setting in and the floor was better than nothing.

That's when Mary noticed the man with the crumpled tie. He was stretched out a few feet away, staring up at the ceiling.

"Comfortable?" she joked.

He snorted, as she expected him to. His gruffness was funny to Mary, who could be gruff herself at times.

He sat up and shoved his back against the wall. "How'd the hotel search go?" he asked, pointing to the phone a few feet away. "I heard you on the phone. Sounded like you were really making progress."

Mary laughed. "I couldn't help but think of Mary and Joseph on Christmas Eve, looking for a room. They ended up in a barn. I guess the airport's not so bad."

The guy nodded and laughed for the first time. "That's a good way to look at it." He held out his hand to shake. "My name's Joseph, and that's exactly how I feel. Like Joseph and Mary. Shut out."

Mary smiled. "This night gets more interesting by the minute. My name's Mary."

The guy's mouth dropped. "No way. Really?"

Mary nodded. "Too weird, huh?"

Joseph grinned wryly. "Now all we need is a newborn baby and we could have our own little nativity scene right here in the flipping airport."

A pregnant woman across from Joseph smirked. "Don't even say it."

They all laughed and Joseph shoved his briefcase under his head for a pillow. He rolled over, and with a sharp flip of his hand, he waved good night to Mary and the pregnant woman. In less than a minute, he was snoring.

At that moment, from the corner of her eye, Mary spotted a little redhead. She looked up and there was the girl exiting the bathroom!

Mary jumped up and bolted after her. "Hey!"

She ran up to the little girl, who was walking toward a water fountain. The girl stopped and turned around. Sure enough, she was wearing the two-toned green-and-white shoes!

Mary bent down. "Where are your parents?"

The little girl's green eyes narrowed and her fingers went to her lips. She ran her fingers along the seam of her mouth, as though zipping up her lips.

"You're not supposed to talk to strangers?" Mary asked. The little girl nodded and walked quickly away.

Not wanting to frighten the child, Mary watched her beeline it down the hallway, her little green corduroy pants and red hair sticking out in the sea of people. Mary waited to see if the girl had a person or a place to go to.

She didn't. She just wandered randomly down the airport hallway. And the farther she wandered, the harder she was to see.

Mary decided to follow her.

The little girl passed a shoe-shine booth, and then a flower shop. But she didn't stop, or even dally, at either place. Suddenly she tilted her head upward, as if having heard or smelled something that interested her. Mary looked around—what had she noticed?

The little girl cocked her head again, but this time in the opposite direction. Her nose went up in the air, as though trying to catch an aroma wafting by with the current of people. She wiggled her nose like a rabbit and then turned around.

Her eyes settled across the way on a store. Mary strained to see what kind of store, but it was too far away. The little girl started toward it and Mary followed her.

A minute later, the child was standing in front of a hamburger stand. The distinct aroma of juicy burgers was strong now, and Mary finally understood what the girl had been doing. She was looking for food. She was hungry.

The child stared up at the pictures of hamburgers on the overhead menu. She reached into her pocket and pulled out a heap of change. As she panned through it, Mary noticed that her hand was filled with pennies. She'd never be able to buy a hamburger with that.

Then Mary noticed a man who was watching the little girl. He seemed nervous, and was glancing around like a thief in a department store. When he bent down, sweat beaded off his brow.

"Are you hungry?" the man asked.

The little girl's head shot up. She

looked the strange man up and down, then zipped up her lip.

"You can talk to me," the man said. "I'm not a stranger, I'm a friend."

The little girl shook her head, narrowed her eyes, and started to walk away.

The man quickly looked around him to make sure no one was looking. Suddenly he reached down to grab the little girl.

Mary lunged toward him. "Let go of her!"

The man froze, his hand just centimeters from the little girl's shoulder. He looked at Mary, fear in his eyes.

"Leave her alone. It's obvious she doesn't know you and doesn't want to talk to you."

The crowd of people at the hamburger stand turned around and stared at the man. The cashier clenched his jaw and motioned for the man to leave the establishment. The man scurried off down the hallway.

Mary leaned down to the little girl. "I know you shouldn't talk to strangers, but maybe I can find a policeman to help you find your parents. Would you like that?"

The little girl shook her head and pointed at the food.

"You want a hamburger?"

She shook her head again and pointed to the farthest picture on the right.

Mary laughed. "Okay, a cheeseburger!"

The little girl smiled and handed Mary the pennies in her hand. Mary shook her head.

"You keep those for another time. I'll buy your cheeseburger, okay?" The little girl nodded, and Mary smiled. "After that, we'll find your parents."

Suddenly the girl shook her head in frustration, and Mary's brow furrowed. "You don't want to find your parents?"

The cashier at the hamburger stand suggested, "Maybe they abandoned her?"

The little girl shook her head again.

"Maybe she's an orphan," he said.

Once more, she shook her head.

"Are you lost?" Mary asked.

The little girl nodded.

"So you do need to find your parents?"

Irritated, the girl finally spoke. "No. I don't need to find them, because they're not here."

"Where are they?" Mary asked.

The little girl rolled her eyes. "At home, silly."

Mary exchanged a look with the cashier, who was smiling at the little girl's brassiness. "I don't understand," Mary said. "Why are they at home, and you're not?"

The girl sighed. "Because I don't ever fly with them. I always fly alone."

Mary was shocked. "Alone? So this isn't an accident?"

The little girl shook her head, and Mary tried to wipe the amazement from her face. Mary's parents hadn't let her fly alone until she had graduated from high school! This girl couldn't have completed first grade.

"But why are you flying alone?" Mary insisted.

"It's a long story. Do we have to go into it?" demanded the little girl.

Mary put her hand on the little girl's shoulder. "If I'm going to help you, then yes, we do."

"I don't need your help. I've got money."

Mary laughed. "You may be smart, but if you don't know that a handful of pennies won't buy you a meal, then you haven't learned to count."

"Yes, I have." She held up her hand and smiled proudly. "Seventy-eight cents. I can buy a McDonald's cheeseburger."

Mary pulled the little girl's ear. "But this isn't McDonald's. Now let me get you a hamburger."

"Cheeseburger," the child corrected.

"Right. A cheeseburger. And then you'll explain to me why a seven-year-old child would ever be allowed to fly alone."

"Six-year-old."

"Even more insane."

"And I'm not poor, for the record. I gave away my money to a nun in the other terminal."

Mary smiled at the unexpected news. "That was sweet of you."

"My parents can deduct it at tax time."

Mary stared at her. Was this kid for real? "And what about eating?"

The girl pulled out an ATM card. "I have plastic."

Mary looked at the card and suddenly felt like she'd been played by a child far more sophisticated than herself. "Then why am I buying?"

The child slipped the card back into her pocket. Then she puffed out her lip and blinked her eyes rapidly like a miniature damsel in distress. "Pretty please?"

Mary raised a brow at the child's precociousness and stepped up to the counter. She looked at the menu and grinned. One thing she knew for certain: no sugar for this kid.

FOUR

The little girl, whose name was Emily, ate her cheeseburger slowly, savoring the smoky taste and talking between bites. Mary was fascinated by what she was learning.

"So you live in Buffalo with your mother?"

Emily nodded and swallowed. "Yeah. We have so much snow right now that the icicles on our roof touch the top of the snowbank."

Mary smiled. "I know. I live in Buffalo, too. We have seven feet of snow in our front yard."

Emily nibbled at a piece of cheese that had dripped down the side of the bun.

"That's taller than a big man."

"You're right. That's the size of a large NBA basketball player."

"Yeah. That's big!"

Mary wiped a sesame seed from Emily's chin. "So why isn't your mom with you now?"

"Because I'm going to see my dad. They're divorced."

Mary nodded. She was beginning to understand. "So your dad lives in one city and you and your mom live in another?"

"You're quick."

"Where is he?" Mary asked.

"California," the little girl said. "The Bear State. That's why there's a bear on their state flag."

Mary laughed. "I'm going to California, too. It's where my family lives, in Glenoak. Where does your dad live?"

"Los Feliz. That's near Hollywood, on the northeastern edge, in Los Angeles. Not to be confused with East LA."

Mary stole one of Emily's fries and popped it in her mouth. "So tell me this, Emily. Aren't your parents afraid of letting you fly all alone—especially when therc's a layover in a big airport like this?"

Emily shook her head. "This is my fifth time flying alone. I'm a pro."

"But aren't they worried that you could get lost?"

"No, because I have a guardian."

Mary sat up, confused. "A guardian? You do?"

Emily nodded. "The airline assigns guardians to kids like me."

"Then where's your guardian?"

"I wandered off from the group."

"The group?" Mary asked.

"Of kids like me."

Mary was astounded. "You mean there are a lot of kids who fly alone, without parents?"

Emily rolled her eyes. "Why are you so worried? It's not a big deal. I just didn't want to be supervised, so I snuck off. I know where my gate is."

Mary shook her head. "It *is* a big deal. There are bad people everywhere, and in an airport nobody's looking out for anyone but themselves. I don't mean to scare you, but that man who wanted to buy you a hamburger really wanted to kidnap you."

Emily took a voracious bite of her burger. "I can take care of myself. If he'd touched me, I would have kicked him right where it hurts. I'm the toughest person in my family. I'm taking karate. When I get kicked, I don't cry. I only cry when I need something."

Mary leaned over. "Listen, Emily. I'm the toughest person in my family, too, but it's taken some hard knocks to make me realize that I can't always take care of myself. I need other people. And so do you. You're six years old! You shouldn't be wandering around alone in an airport. So as soon as you finish your burger, we're going to go find your guardian."

Before Emily could protest, Mary felt a tap on her shoulder. She turned around and found herself staring eyeball to eyeball with the scowling bathroom attendant. A police officer stood next to the woman.

"This is her, Officer," the attendant said. "She's been stalking this little girl."

Mary jumped up. "What? No, no . . . you've got it all wrong. This is Emily—"

The attendant cut her off. "I thought you said her name was Hillary."

Mary shook her head, sighing. "I was improvising. I didn't have time to—"

The officer stepped in. "To what? To make up a better lie?"

"N-No . . . ," Mary stuttered.

The policeman waited for her to finish. "Don't be nervous, miss, just tell the truth."

Mary nodded, taking a deep breath. "I was on the telephone, and this little girl, Emily, approached me. She asked me where the bathroom was, and I pointed it out to her. When she walked away, I suddenly realized that she wouldn't have asked me for help unless she was alone. So I followed her to see if she needed anything, but this woman here wouldn't even let me talk to her."

The attendant narrowed her eyes, wary of Mary's story. "Listen, miss, there are children all over this airport without their parents, and people like you come along all the time and snatch them right up."

The officer looked at Mary, trying to gauge the verity of her story. "You sound like a nice kid, but how do I know that you don't have ulterior motives?"

Just then, the cashier from the burger stand walked up. He explained the scenario he had witnessed. "This child was in danger, and this young lady here stepped in and saved her. Then she bought the kid a burger, and asked me to call airport security for help."

The officer looked at the little girl. "Is that right, sweetie?"

Emily shook her head, to Mary's horror. "My name's not sweetie."

The officer leaned down. "Then what is it, honey?"

"It's not honey, either."

Suddenly a security guard pulled up in a blue cart and jumped out. He spotted the officer and ran up to him. "I'm here about the lost little girl. Is that her?" He pointed at Emily.

The officer nodded. "Yes. So you were paged?"

The security guard nodded and pointed to the cashier. "Johnny paged me. Said a young lady had asked for assistance with a lost child."

The officer smiled and held out his hand to Mary, who shook it. "Congratulations on a job well done. You took a risk to save a child, and in this day and age, that's a real act of courage and compassion."

Mary shook her head. "Anybody would have done the same thing."

The bathroom attendant, whose tight posture had begun to loosen, smiled. "No, most people wouldn't have done the same thing. I'm sorry I didn't trust you, but you can't imagine the kind of freaks who pass through this place. This is not a safe place for a child."

Mary nodded. "I understand. You were just trying to do your job. It's nice to know people like you are out there watching after kids like Emily."

"Same with you," the woman said, patting Mary on the back.

The officer clapped his hands together as though he were a teacher ending a class. "Well, I guess it's time to find Emily's guardian."

Mary smiled. "And it's time for me to get some sleep. I'm exhausted!" She bent down and pulled Emily's ear. "It's time to say goodbye, Emily."

But Emily didn't return the smile. Instead, she opened her mouth and let out the loudest scream Mary had ever heard. Tears rolled down her cheeks as though her eyes were faucets that had been turned on with the simple twist of a hand. "I WANT MARY!"

Mary looked at Emily in surprise as the entire terminal turned to see what trauma had occurred. *Wow, this kid really does know how to cry when she wants something,* Mary thought.

The officer's control over the situation suddenly dissipated. Handling criminals was one thing, but handling kids . . . He sighed and looked at Mary. His smile was desperate, his tone pleading.

"You wouldn't want to help baby-sit, would you?"

Mary leaned down and shot a scolding look at Emily. "I know your tricks because I have them, too, and they won't work on me. The next time you even sniffle will be the last time you see me. Got it?"

Emily shut her mouth and grinned. "It's a deal!"

What had Mary gotten herself into now?

FIVE

The officer led Mary and Emily through a set of double glass doors. Inside was a large group of children and one exhausted flight attendant. As soon as Emily was inside, the attendant spotted her and jumped up.

"Emily!" she cried, with a mixture of joy and relief. "Thank God somebody found you. I was so terrified!"

Mary looked crossly at •the woman, failing to hold her tongue. "So how is it, exactly, that a child under your supervision could get lost in an airport? It seems pretty negligent to me. What if Emily had been kidnapped? As a matter of fact, she almost was."

The woman, who'd been smiling until now, snapped back at Mary. "How dare you blame me for this situation? Would you look around you? There are seventeen kids in this room, and only one of me to go around!"

Mary shrugged. "Then I guess you should demand that your airline hire seventeen of you."

The woman put her hands on her hips and laid into Mary. "I already have. In fact, I'm on our union board, and I demand it at every meeting. But when I take the concern to management, do you think they care? I'm just a lowly stewardess whose purpose in life is to get yelled at every fifteen minutes by self-righteous customers like you."

Mary's mouth was frozen in an open gape. She swallowed hard, realizing that she didn't have a comeback. She started to apologize, but the woman wasn't finished with her diatribe.

"In case you haven't noticed, it's Christmas Eve, and these kids are devastated to be spending it away from their parents. Which makes them a bit more emotional than usual. Which is why Emily was able to sneak off: I was chasing a bawling runaway."

Mary tried to jump in again, but the woman was on a roll. "And another thing—do you think I'm going to get to stretch out on the floor tonight? That I'm going to get on a flight tomorrow so that I can spend Christmas with my family? No! I'll be dropping these kids off and picking up a whole new group to take back across the country. So I'd appreciate your assistance rather than your attitude."

Mary waited to make sure the woman was finished. Then she quietly said, "I'm sorry."

The woman started up again, then froze, realizing that Mary had actually apologized. She looked at Mary, whose eyes were sincere and apologetic. "It's okay," she sighed.

The policeman, who until now had let the argument run its course, stepped in. "Listen, ladies, it's been a difficult night. The best thing we can do is work together. It's the only thing that will get us through it."

Mary nodded and looked at the woman. Her eyes were ringed with dark circles, as if she hadn't slept in several days. "I shouldn't have jumped to conclusions, and I certainly didn't mean to attack you like that. I guess we're all a bit irritable right now. The important thing is that Emily's safe," Mary conceded.

The woman nodded. "Yes, that is the most important thing." She took another breath, as though trying to set her emotions aside. "Are you the one who found her?"

Mary nodded, and the policeman introduced the two women. The flight attendant's name was Jackie.

"Now then . . . ," the policeman said. "I have another emergency to attend to. Can the two of you handle the situation alone?"

Mary nodded and looked at Jackie. "Absolutely. I'm here to help."

Jackie smiled as the policeman left. "I appreciate it. The truth is, I do feel guilty for losing Emily. I don't know what I would have done if you hadn't found her. . . ."

The two women looked down at Emily, who rolled her eyes. "I'm just fine!"

Just then, a little boy pulled on Mary's leg. She bent down and smiled at the black-haired child.

"Did you need something?"

The little boy nodded. "When are the planes leaving?"

Mary sighed and shook her head. "Not for a while, I'm afraid."

He pursed his lips and frowned, agitated. "Am I going to be home for Christmas?"

Mary sat down on the floor and patted the space next to her. "I sure hope so. But if we're not, we'll be here, together, and everything will be fine."

His eyes filled with tears. "But everything's not fine. Everything's awful!"

Mary put her arm around him. "Tell me what's bad, and maybe I can help fix something."

"All my presents are under the tree, and I won't be home to open them."

Mary nodded. "But the good news is that your parents won't let anybody else open them. So they'll be waiting for you. And when everybody else is done opening their presents tomorrow, you'll come home and still have something to look forward to."

The little boy wasn't impressed. In fact,

Mary's words seemed to agitate him even more. His pursed lips turned into a pout, and his pout turned into an all-out cry. "But that means that they'll open their presents without me!"

Uh-oh. I got myself into this one, didn't I? Mary thought.

She shook her head, backtracking. "No . . . they won't. They won't really open them without you."

"But you said . . ."

"You're right, I did. I spoke too soon, without thinking clearly. I was wrong. Now that I think about it, no parents would open presents without all their children being there."

He sniffled, big tears rolling down his cheeks. "Then why did you say it?"

Mary started to explain, then realized there was a better way to calm the boy. "Let's come back to the presents later. Tell me something else that's bad about being here."

"I'm lonely. All the other kids have friends."

Mary looked at Emily, who'd been listening to the exchange. Emily crossed her arms. She knew what was coming.

"You want me to be this kid's friend?" she said.

Mary raised a parental eyebrow, shooting a look at the unyielding girl. "No. I want him to be your friend. Because you don't have any."

Emily's eyes widened in surprise. She hadn't expected Mary to say that. But it was true. Emily was a loner. She did things on her own. And sometimes that got lonely.

The little boy smiled and sat up. He patted the space on the other side of him. "Come sit by me. I'm Skyler."

Emily dropped down next to him. "Skyler, huh? That's a pretty cool name."

"What's your name?" he asked.

"Emily." Emily held out her hand to shake, and suddenly Mary realized who Emily reminded her of. Ruthie! She was just like Ruthie: independent, precocious, cynical, and mischievous.

Mary looked around the room at the other children. Contrary to what Skyler had said, they weren't all hanging out in groups of friends. In reality, each of them looked alienated, frightened, and alone.

Most of their faces were puffy from crying, and their eyes looked exhausted. Yet none of them were sleeping. Maybe the floor was too hard? Or maybe they needed an adult to make them feel safe enough to close their eyes?

Mary spotted a crying girl and started to get up, but as soon as she moved, Skyler grabbed her hand. "Don't go."

His hand was ice cold. She looked at him. His nose was running, too. She leaned down again.

"Are you sick?"

He shook his head.

"Then why is your nose running?"

He shrugged. "Because it's cold."

Mary looked around the room. Almost every single kid was huddled into a ball, as though trying to keep warm. Mary was lucky she had worn such a heavy coat. But even her hands were starting to get chilly. And her feet felt like icicles. *There must be something wrong with the heating system*, she thought.

Mary kissed Skyler's head and promised him and Emily that she'd be right back. She walked over to Jackie, who was reading nursery rhymes to a crying child.

"Are there any blankets available? These kids are freezing."

Jackie shook her head. "Not nearby. The ones from our plane were sent to the laundry already, and the plane we would have boarded is closed."

Mary frowned. "You said there aren't any nearby. How far away are they?"

Jackie thought about it. "Well, there's a storage facility on the other side of the terminal. That's where our airline's blankets are kept. But you'd have to find somebody to let you in. If I could get away, I could help you, but I'm legally obligated to stay here."

Mary nodded. "Could you page somebody from the airline and ask them to let me in?"

Jackie sighed. "If it were a normal night, yes. But we're so understaffed right now that I can't page anyone unless it's a dire emergency. Your best bet is standing in line at the check-in desk, but I don't think it'll be easy."

Mary thought about the long line she'd stood in before. And the poor service. And the angry people . . .

On the other hand, these children were cold. Very cold.

She stood up and looked at the kids. "How would everybody like to have a blanket?" she shouted.

Suddenly all the children's sad faces lit up. "Yay!" they shouted in unison. Mary looked at Jackie, who shrugged, hoping that Mary could fulfill their expectations. Mary grinned and ran out the double doors.

SIX

The end of the line was no more appealing the second time around. So Mary plowed right through the angry people again—but this time with a good reason. The right reason.

She leaned her elbows on top of the check-in desk and waved urgently at the agent. Without looking up from his computer console, he shook his head. "Get in line."

Mary didn't budge, but instead slammed the palm of her hand against the top of the desk. That got his attention. He glared at her. She smiled.

"I'm not here to get my money back—"

He went back to his typing. "Good."

A woman in line leaned over and looked at the console. "Have you upped me to first class yet or what?"

Mary slammed her palm against the desk again. The man stopped his typing and gave her all his irritated attention. "Do you mind?" he hissed.

Mary smiled again. "I'm here to help."

Mistrusting her words, the man hissed again. "Help? You're here to help?"

Mary nodded. "That's right."

The man stood up, leaned over, and yelled, "Then stop banging your hand on my countertop!"

A man behind her spoke up. "And stop cutting in line. You cut in line a couple hours ago. I remember!"

There was a grumbling that reverberated down the line. Mary could sense that she was about to be mobbed if she didn't win the crowd over quickly. She turned around and held up a hand, trying to silence them.

"Listen, I'm sorry for cutting before. But this time it's not for selfish reasons. It's to help children who are stranded here without their parents. So if you'll just give me a minute, I'll be gone in no time."

The group hemmed and hawed a bit, then exchanged glances with one another. Finally, the man spoke up. "All right. But hurry up. We're tired of waiting in this line!"

Mary smiled. "Thanks." Then she turned back to the check-in attendant. He was smiling wryly.

"Thanks for the rousing speech," he said, his voice dripping with sarcasm. "Nothing like rallying the troops in a time of war. Truly, you deserve a medal."

Mary reached out her hand and touched his. "No, I don't. You do."

The man sat up in surprise at her words. He looked at her, uncertain if she was being sincere. But he could tell by the look in Mary's eyes that she was. His cynical expression faded. He pushed out a smile. "I've been working fifteen hours straight, and it feels really good to hear you say that. Thank you."

Mary nodded. "You're welcome."

"Now what can I do for you?"

Mary launched into her idea like a salesperson making a pitch. "I know there are blankets on all the planes, and I'm sure that there are blankets in storage somewhere. I'd like to organize a group to gather them up and hand them out, since we'll all be sleeping here tonight."

The man sighed—not because he didn't like the idea, but because he knew it would take a lot of time. Time that he didn't have. "That's a really nice gesture, but it would be a lot of work. Look at all these people I have to deal with. I just don't have time to organize a blanket party."

Mary shook her head. "You don't have to. You just have to get someone to open a door and trust that I'm here to help."

The man looked at her, uncertain. "Trust a complete stranger at a time like this?"

Mary retorted, "Isn't this the right time to trust? It's the holiday season."

He looked at his watch. "Listen. If I can get a replacement over here, I'll help you out. But it may be an hour or more."

Mary considered his offer, then thought about the kids, cold and afraid, in a foreign place. An hour was an eternity to them.

She looked back at the people in the line. They were all glaring at her. Maybe she could win them over a second time.

Maybe she could find enough blankets for them as well. Suddenly Mary's brain was spinning. Why not find enough blankets for everyone in the entire terminal?

She waved her hand at them. "Is anyone interested in helping me get blankets to pass out—not just to the children, but to you and your families as well?"

An irate woman in the middle of the line screamed, her voice as sharp as a razor blade. "Blankets? I'm here to get a refund! Now get out of our line!"

A man just behind her barked in response, "I'm gonna sue! I paid two thousand dollars for my seat!"

A third lady leaped into the ring. "Two grand a pop, and they don't have enough money to put us in a hotel? That's nothing short of thievery!"

Mary was fascinated as she watched the group grow angrier. They were no different from animals, like a pack of wolves looking for prey. *Was I acting like this before?* she wondered. She held up her hand again, and the group fell silent. Mary realized the power she had. She was, at least for now, the group's rational voice.

"I know you don't want to hear this, but there are no hotel rooms. I've called all over the city myself, and not a single hotel has a vacancy. I even asked to stay in janitor's closets. So don't blame the airline, and especially not this poor man." Mary motioned to the attendant at the desk. "He's not keeping you out of a hotel room because his company's cheap. The rooms simply do not exist. This situation is not the airline's fault. In fact, if you go to the other terminals, you'll find that every airline in Chicago is in the same predicament. They can't control the weather. God does. And on Christmas Eve, He certainly knows what He's doing—right?"

Mary waited for someone to heckle her. But nobody did. In fact, the line was completely silent. She looked around the room and realized that even the people on the floor and in the chairs were listening to her. She smiled.

"Maybe there's a lesson for all of us to learn tonight. Just two hours ago, I was ready to punch anyone who got in my way. Now I've realized that patience and generosity go a lot further than anger and irritation at a time like this. And I've also realized there are people much less fortunate than me tonight."

Mary looked out the window at the raging storm. "There are actually people outside in that storm, without a place to go tonight. They could die." Mary let the words sink in. "At least we have a roof over our heads. . . ."

That's when Mary heard a voice that she recognized, coming from the far corner of the room. She looked over and saw Clayton, the curly-haired guy whom she'd run into in the hallway. He was surrounded by young teenagers. He smiled and stood up.

"I'll help you gather blankets. As a matter of fact, I have a whole group of church youth who are bored out of their minds and too hyper to sleep. Could you use them?"

Mary grinned and nodded. Then she looked at the attendant, hoping he would agree to help. He smiled and nodded. What did he have to lose? He hit his intercom button and requested assistance.

Which is when the truly miraculous

event occurred: the angry woman in line looked at the others and said, "Ah, let's give the poor guy a break."

The barking man nodded. "What the heck? Let's leave him alone."

Suddenly the entire line dispersed, and the attendant was finally free to do the one thing he'd wanted to do all night: he laid his head down on the countertop and closed his eyes.

As Mary waited for assistance to arrive, she felt yet another tap from a stranger. She turned around and saw the Governor's wife, who was holding out her thick fur coat. "Maybe this will warm a few of the children."

Mary smiled and thanked the woman for the offer. "I'm sorry for yelling at you earlier," the woman said. "It's amazing how a crisis can either bring out the worst in us, or the best. I was supposed to be in Los Angeles with my husband tonight for the annual lighting of the Christmas tree. It's my favorite time of the year, and I'm devastated to miss it. I let my anger overcome me when I should have been using this event to unite people. You've been an inspiration. If you're ever in Sacramento and need a place to stay, I'll make sure you have a room."

Mary smiled. "My family lives in Glenoak, so I might just take you up on it."

Just then, a woman arrived with a large ring of keys as Clayton and the youth group joined up with Mary. The scavenger hunt was about to begin!

SEVEN

The woman led Mary, Clayton, and the teens into a large storage facility. Unopened boxes were piled against every inch of wall space. The woman pointed to a corner.

"I think the blankets are in those boxes. Unfortunately, Jeffrey has been deployed to deal with a crisis in the shipping yard, so you'll have to figure it out on your own."

Mary's jaw dropped. "You mean the man who oversees this facility is outside in this weather?"

The woman nodded. "He receives all of our airline's incoming freight. Plastic spoons, napkins, food trays, blankets, pillows, magazines . . ."

Mary shook her head. "Wow, you people work really hard. I had no idea."

Clayton nodded, then asked the woman a question. "You said he receives pillows, too. Can we snag some?"

The woman shrugged. "I was told to trust you kids, so that's what I'm going to do. Now if you'll excuse me, there's been a report that water is leaking into a hallway from under a locked door. I've got to go open it and hope that it's just a leaking faucet rather than a collapsing roof." And with that, the woman was off.

Mary looked at Clayton and rubbed her hands together. "Thanks for your help."

He smiled. "I knew I'd run into you again."

The youth group started laughing and making kissing sounds. Clayton turned around. "All right, all right, let's get to work. You see all the X-Acto knives on that shelf? Very carefully use them to open the boxes the woman pointed to. Let's find those blankets!"

Mary pointed to a row of dollies in the center of the room. "Once we find the right boxes, we can load three at a time on the dollies. And don't forget the pillows!"

Clayton added, "Whoever finds the blankets first gets a pizza on me."

The kids jumped into action. In less than a minute, they had a prize-winner.

Like kids in a candy store, Mary, Clayton, and the youth group pushed their loaded dollies into the terminal hallway. Exhausted travelers watched them with curiosity, surprised to find themselves smiling at one o'clock in the morning.

The group's spirit was infectious as they rolled into the gate. People who had heard Mary's speech perked up at the sight of her, the corners of their mouths turning up as their eyes took note of the boxes filled with blankets.

As soon as the kids began handing out the blankets, the atmosphere in the room began to change dramatically. Even the cantankerous woman from the line broke into a smile when Mary handed her the blanket. She wrapped it around her shoulders and nuzzled her face into the soft cotton, delighted.

Mary looked at Clayton and laughed. "There's something about blankets that calm people down. Suddenly the floor doesn't seem as bad as it did before!"

But if Mary thought things were good when the blankets were given out, she was really in for a surprise when the pillows were revealed. The travelers didn't just smile, they stood up and cheered!

When Mary and her new friends wheeled the last boxes into the children's room, she almost cried at the response. The sad, empty eyes of the kids suddenly filled with hope. And Jackie, who had heroically kept her eyes open for the twenty-second hour straight, did cry.

Mary raised her hands. "Not only do we have blankets for you little rugrats, we have pillows!"

The children couldn't believe it. They started bouncing and chattering and rocking back and forth.

Mary had a good idea. "Okay, everyone, I want you to put your hands together and stretch out your arms like this." She demonstrated, turning her own arms into the shape of a circle, like a basketball hoop.

The kids did as they were told, excited to play whatever unknown game Mary was proposing. Then Mary grabbed a pillow and motioned for Clayton and the youth group to grab pillows as well. They did.

"Now then, we're going to play some basketball. You don't get a pillow until one of us is able to get it through your hoop."

The kids started laughing, and Jackie was relieved to have the responsibility of their well-being taken off her hands for a moment.

Mary continued. "Now this is a group effort. So if the person shooting at your hoop is a bad shot, like Clayton here"— she elbowed him and the kids laughed— "then you have to help out by moving your hoop so the pillow goes through. Okay?"

They all nodded, and Mary looked at the youth group. "You all ready?" They nodded. "Let the games begin!"

Suddenly the teens were tossing, jumping, hooking, ally-ooping, and banking against little heads, and best of all, everyone was laughing.

In the meantime, Mary was placing blankets beside each excited child. By the time everyone had "won" their pillows, the blankets were ready and waiting for the tired little bodies.

Mary put her arm around Clayton. She

looked at the children. "Now without further ado, let's do the one thing we've been waiting to do all night: sleep!"

Jackie started clapping, and Clayton joined in. Even a few of the youth group responded favorably. But the children didn't like the idea. In fact, they hated it. To Mary's surprise, a new round of crying began, which turned into a frenzy of wails, whimpers, and howls of "I want my mommy!"

Mary looked at Clayton in shock: this was the last response she had expected. But why didn't she expect it? No child wanted to sleep without his or her parents, even with a nice, warm blanket.

She sighed and looked at Jackie, who appeared haggard and was shaking her head. *Okay, Mary, improvise.*

Mary climbed up onto a chair and held out her arms like a choir conductor. She began moving her right hand up, down, and across, in the shape of a triangle—just as an orchestra director would do. She moved her hand passionately as the cries grew and grew, then backed away gently as they mellowed.

One by one, the children stopped crying and watched her. Mary continued to conduct the cries until the last child fell silent. Then in one sweeping motion, she threw her hand around in a half circle and made a fist, like a conductor ending a piece of music.

The kids started laughing again, and Mary dropped down onto the seat and leaned in. "Let's all talk about what we want for Christmas."

The children nodded, and Mary turned to Emily. "Emily, what do you want for Christmas?"

Emily sighed. "I want to go home."

Mary raised an eyebrow at her. "Try again."

Emily looked at her, and Mary crossed her arms. Emily rolled her eyes, finally giving in and starting the game off as Mary wanted her to. "I asked for a scooter."

The kids all started shouting. Some yelled, "Me too, me too!" and others shouted, "I already have one!"

Emily turned to Skyler. "What do you want for Christmas, Skyler?"

Skyler bit his thumbnail, nervous to address the room. Emily put her arm around him. "It's okay," she whispered.

"You can tell me what you want, and I'll tell them."

Skyler whispered in Emily's ear, and she looked at the group. "Skyler wants a basketball."

A boy across the room jumped up. "I want a football!"

Suddenly Mary had a thought: she'd bought a basketball for Ruthie for Christmas, and it was here at the airport, in her luggage. . . .

What if I pulled the presents that I bought for my family out of my luggage and passed them out here, to the children? Wait . . . what if we all did that? she thought excitedly.

Mary leaned over and whispered to Clayton. His eyes lit up.

"Not a bad idea," he whispered. "But how would we get to our luggage?"

Mary shrugged. "If we could get blankets for an entire terminal, we could get anything."

Clayton nodded, then leaned over and whispered to one of his youth members. The kid grinned and passed the idea on. Within seconds, the youth group was filing back out the double doors.

EIGHT

An hour later, Mary had tracked down a pilot who had served in the military with her grandfather. He managed to unlock another door for her, Clayton, and the youth group. Just inside was a huge holding area for luggage. Thousands of bags surrounded them, partitioned off into separate areas.

The pilot smiled at the group, then led them to a muscular man who wore a wide leather support around his back. He clapped the man on the shoulder.

"Pete. I want you to meet Mary Camden. Served with her grandfather in the military. Got good blood, the Camdens. Honest and reliable."

Mary smiled and waved at Pete. Pete nodded. Then he turned back to the pilot. "So what can I do for you, Jim?"

Jim pointed at the youth group. "These kids need to find their luggage and retrieve some gifts. Plan on handing the gifts out to some stranded children."

Mary handed Pete a list of luggage descriptions, flight numbers, and names. He looked it over, then shouted at a group of men who were stacking luggage in a corner. The men stopped their work and started toward Pete.

Pete showed the men the list, then asked them to show the kids to their luggage. The men kicked it into high gear. Within seconds, they were sifting quickly through bags, pulling out the right ones, and tossing them into a new pile.

The pilot thanked Pete, who nodded and went back to work. Then he turned to Mary. He rubbed his chin as he looked her up and down, like a sergeant inspecting a new cadet. Finally, he smiled. She'd definitely made the grade. "I'll report back to the Colonel that he's got a fine granddaughter."

Mary grinned and playfully saluted him. "And I'll report back that he's got a fine friend. Thanks for all your help. We couldn't have done it without you."

"No problem, kiddo." He winked and started for the door. Then he stopped and turned around. There was a twinkle in his eye. "Can you guess what I get to do now?"

Mary feigned a scowl. "Sleep?"

He laughed and threw his arm up victoriously into the air. "That's right! Sleep!"

Mary laughed and turned to Clayton. But Clayton was distracted. He was looking off in another area of the room. Far away, clear across the holding facility, was a Dumpster. And in that Dumpster was an object that Clayton found very intriguing.

"What are you looking at?" Mary asked.

Clayton started walking toward it. As he got closer, he started running. Curious, Mary took off running after him. And as she got closer, she realized why he was so excited.

Sitting in the garbage bin was a large

Christmas tree. Its green branches were heavy with fake silver icicles, and a star decorated the top.

Just then, a man walked by, noticing the two inspecting the tree. "It's from our employee Christmas party."

Clayton looked at the guy, who was already out the door. "Can we have it?" he yelled.

From the next room, they heard him yell back, "Sure!"

Mary looked at Clayton, who was smiling at her. "This is too good to be true," she said, almost breathless.

Clayton held her eyes. "You're too good to be true, Mary."

The comment took Mary off guard. She felt her cheeks redden, and she reached into the bin for the tree, relieved to have a distraction. Clayton touched her hand.

"I know we'll probably never see each other again, but . . . the more time I spend with you, the better I like you."

Mary smiled and met his eyes. "You know what? That's a really nice thing to hear. I doubt myself a lot."

"Why? All I see is an incredible, powerful young woman with an amazing ability to inspire people. You've inspired me."

Mary bit her lip and looked away. *I feel like I'm cheating on Robbie right now.*

Clayton pulled his hand back. "You have a boyfriend, don't you?"

Mary looked at him and nodded. "Yes. Sort of . . . I don't know what I have. It's one of those on-again, off-again things."

Clayton's gaze was strong and steady. "Is it off now?"

Mary shook her head, amazed at how difficult it was to be honest with him. "No."

He smiled again and reached back into the Dumpster. "Well, he's a lucky guy."

Mary smiled, a bit of her mischievous nature returning. "I'll tell him that."

Clayton laughed and helped Mary pull the tree out. They set it down between them, then looked at one another once more.

"So do you live in California?" Mary asked.

He shook his head. "New York."

Mary smiled at the coincidence. "Me too."

Clayton smiled. "Maybe we'll bump

into each other again back there."

Mary laughed. "Yeah, maybe."

Suddenly there was a shout from across the room. One of the kids had spotted the tree. And in less than thirty seconds, everyone had abandoned the gift hunt and was running across the room toward Mary and Clayton. Something about the sight of a Christmas tree on this long, strange night was magical.

"Can I carry it?" one of the teens asked.

Mary nodded. "I think you'll need some help."

Fifteen hands went up. Mary reached down, grabbed a wad of paper from the floor, and threw it as high as she could. "Whoever catches it can help carry the tree. . . ."

The entire group jumped, climbing over one another to snatch the white ball from the air. The tallest boy almost had it, but a shove knocked his legs out from under him. He tipped the paper ball, and it ricocheted backward, falling right into the hands of the shortest girl in the group. She looked at it in shock.

"I got it," she peeped.

Mary rustled her hair. "Then you win."

The girl pushed her glasses up on her nose, closed her eyes, and jumped ever so slightly. "Cool," she whispered, and the whole group laughed as the two kids walked off with the tree.

NINE

As the youth group paraded through the terminal for the second time, they noticed that most of the travelers were sound asleep and covered with blankets, their heads comfortably perched atop pillows. However, the few remaining insomniacs found their interest piqued by the gift-laden youngsters who were marching by. A few of the sleepless passengers even decided to follow the group.

Moments later, the two teens carrying the Christmas tree walked through the double doors into the children's room. The exhausted children's eyes widened in happy surprise. Emily stood up and shouted in glee. "Mary Camden, you have outdone yourself!"

Mary walked in and looked at Emily. "Oh, you just wait, Miss Emily. The Christmas party has only begun, and the night is about to get even better!"

Mary turned and motioned toward the double doors with a broad sweep of both arms. "Presenting Clayton and the Central Valley Youth Group!"

The doors swung open, and Clayton led the youth group inside. A loud gasp of awe went up as the children saw the colorful presents. They watched in anticipation as the gifts were laid on the floor beneath the Christmas tree.

Pointing to the present in her hand, Mary leaned down and whispered to Skyler. "This is the present you want to pick. Okay?"

Skyler nodded fervently and Mary winked a secret wink as she walked up and laid the gift beneath the tree.

Then she turned around to the group, who fell silent.

"Before any of you children get to pick out your gifts, there's one person who has a special gift waiting for her. This is the person who's stayed with you all day and all night, from the first minute you climbed off your plane until now. Can anybody tell me who that is?"

A loud shout of "Jackie!" went up, and Mary nodded.

"Let's all say thank you to Jackie."

The children all shouted their thanks, and Mary walked to Jackie and placed the present she had bought for her own mother in Jackie's lap. "Open it," she said.

Jackie smiled and began opening the present. Then she smiled and held up the gift. It was a gold paperweight, engraved with THANKS FOR BEING THE BEST MOM.

She read the words out loud and laughed. "In a way, these are my kids, aren't they?"

Mary nodded. "We really appreciate all you've done."

Jackie's eyes filled with tears. "Thank you."

Mary hugged Jackie, then turned back to the children. She noticed that a large group of onlookers had gathered just inside the door. Among them was the Governor's wife, who was smiling.

Mary waved, then returned her attention to the children. "One by one, starting with Skyler, each of you can go up and pick out a present."

Excited, Skyler looked at Mary and returned the secret wink. Then he ran up to the tree and picked out Mary's gift. By the time he had run back to his seat, the paper was already trailing behind him on the floor. He jumped up and down in excitement: "A basketball!"

Within minutes, paper was flying across the room, footballs were slamming into walls, and heads were ducking for cover. Mary looked around the room at the delighted children, realizing that in most households across America, children were sound asleep in their beds. She smiled, noting that this was a Christmas none of these children would ever forget. In fact, it was a Christmas she'd never forget.

She turned to Clayton. "What are you thinking about right now?"

Clayton didn't even pause. "I'm thinking that this is what Christmas is all about. Helping people in times of need, giving gifts out of love instead of obligation. I'm thinking about how far away from the true meaning of Christmas we've gotten, and how right now, we're experiencing it. I feel lucky."

Mary murmured in agreement. "I've learned a real lesson about myself tonight."

Clayton looked at her. "What?"

"I'm not a very patient person. It's one of my biggest faults. I'm impulsive, I jump to conclusions when I shouldn't, and I'm very reactive. But tonight I've proven that I'm capable of having patience, and capable of leading. I always knew that, but I had somehow forgotten. It feels really good. It's the best present anyone could have given me."

Clayton smiled. "I'm glad. You're a great woman, Mary Camden. I'm lucky to have met you."

Mary breathed in a long, happy breath, savoring the moment. Then she climbed back up on the same chair she'd used earlier in the night. But unlike before, the wild energy in the room was almost unstoppable. Nobody even noticed her standing there. So she put her two pinky fingers between her lips and whistled as loud as she could.

The room fell silent.

Mary grinned. "Before we get too caught up in our gifts, why don't we all gather in a circle, hold hands, and sing a song to welcome Christmas?"

Mary motioned toward the adults standing near the door, and smiled at a sleepy Joseph, who had just joined the group. His tie was more wrinkled than ever. "You too!" she said, and the room quickly filled with people. In fact, there were so many people that when they joined hands, they had to form several concentric circles.

Emily raised her hand and Mary called on her. "Yes, Emily?"

"What song are we going to sing?"

Mary laughed. "What else but 'I'll Be Home for Christmas'!"

TEN

The next night, while the Camdens were camped around the Christmas tree watching the minutes tick by, the front door opened and they heard Mary shout, "merry Christmas!"

Eric and Annie ran into the foyer and hugged her like she was a soldier returning from war.

Reverend Camden was confused. "Why didn't you call us to come pick you up?"

Mary raised a mischievous eyebrow. "Because I wanted to surprise you!"

Annie sighed and poked an elbow into Mary's side. "We thought you were still stranded in Chicago." She rolled her eyes, then hugged her eldest daughter. "You're going to give me an ulcer, do you know that?"

Before Mary could respond, she felt a hand grab hers. She turned around and was standing nose to nose with Robbie.

"Why didn't you call me back?" he asked.

"Because I was busy saving the world," she retorted.

"So I'm your second priority?" he joked.

"Since I'm yours, yes," she responded.

He furrowed one brow. "Hey, my comment was a joke," he said.

She grinned and pinched his nose. "So was mine."

"Well, I didn't think it was funny."

Mary rolled her eyes. "Who's sensitive now?"

Annie whacked Mary's head as Eric walked by and whacked Robbie's. "Would you two knock it off?" they said in unison.

Mary threw her arms around Robbie, who kissed her. "We're just joking around," they answered in unison.

Which is when they heard an annoyed sigh from the living room. Ruthie.

"Can I finally open my presents?"

Mary strutted into the living room. "Well, well, look who's more interested in presents than people."

Ruthie held out her hand. "Where's my gift?"

Mary's eyes widened for effect. "I gave it away."

"Nuh-uh."

"Yuh-huh," Mary said. "To a terrified little boy stranded in the Chicago airport."

Simon nodded. "That's cool."

Ruthie rolled her eyes. "Whatever."

Mary picked Ruthie up and tossed her over her shoulder like a sack of potatoes. "So what you get instead is a good tickling!"

As Mary's hand dug into Ruthie's tummy, the little girl started shouting and kicking, emitting an uncontrollable frenzy of laughter.

Mary finally stopped and tossed Ruthie back on the couch. She bent down in front of her and confided, "That's what Christmas is about Ruthie. People."

Ruthie looked at her sister strangely. "Are you sick or something?"

Mary laughed and ran over to the twins. She picked them up, holding one on each hip. "Look at these two beautiful boys," she cooed. When she looked up, Annie and Eric were watching her with cocked heads and big smiles.

"You seem really happy," Eric said.

Annie nodded. "Like you've had a life-changing experience."

Mary kissed the tops of Sam's and David's heads, then sat them back down on the couch. "I have. I've realized that Christmas isn't about presents. It's about love; it's about taking care of the people around us; it's about giving whatever it is that you have to give. And most of all, I've realized that what I have to give is good."

Annie threw her arms around Mary. "I'm so glad you've realized that, Mary." She pulled back and looked at her beautiful daughter. "We've known it all along."

Ruthie picked up a green-and-red cookie and threw it at the two. "Enough already! Let's open presents!"

Matt walked in. He reached down and picked up the crumbled cookie. Popping it in his mouth, he nodded in agreement. "I'll open first."

Christmas at the Camdens' had officially begun.

MATT AND THE KING

ONE

Mary threw her new sweater—a Christmas present from Lucy—on top of the pile of clothes already jammed into her shabby suitcase. She pounded the clothes flat, slammed the lid, and whirled around to face her older brother, who was sprawled on a chair in her room.

"I can't believe you're going to take Robbie to Las Vegas for New Year's Eve!" she cried. "What can you be thinking?"

Matt squirmed in his seat. He'd just stopped in to say goodbye before Mary left for Buffalo. Now he regretted it.

"I'm not *taking* him," replied Matt. "I'm *joining* him. So if you want to blame someone, blame Tony Carr, not me."

"And just who is this Tony Carr?" Mary demanded, hands on her hips.

Matt shrugged. "He's some guy that helped Robbie after Cheryl broke up with him. Tony gave Robbie a place to stay for a few weeks, even invited him to move to Las Vegas with his band."

Mary rolled her eyes. "Great. He's a musician. Probably some player, surrounded by groupies and showgirls."

Matt shook his head, laughing. "Tony Carr is probably a geek with a run-down lounge act. He invited Robbie to Las Vegas because he wanted a friendly face in the audience when he bombs."

"Can't you talk Robbie out of going?" Mary asked.

"I could," Matt said. "But he believes he owes it to Tony to be there for him. Robbie doesn't want to let the guy down."

"But—"

"You should be *thanking* me," said Matt. "I'm the guy who volunteered to go along so Robbie wouldn't have to make the drive alone."

"So he wouldn't have to *have fun* alone is more like it," Mary shot back.

"So what's wrong with having a little

fun on New Year's Eve? Besides, Dad's coming along, too, in case you haven't heard—to keep an eye on *both* of us. And you know Dad. He wouldn't let Robbie get into any trouble . . . or me, unfortunately," Matt added with a roll of his eyes.

"Or maybe he thinks it will be good for Robbie to meet someone else. Maybe he's sick of dealing with our relationship," countered Mary.

"Relationship?" Matt's brow furrowed. He sure had trouble keeping up with his sister's "relationships" these days. One day she was Robbie's girlfriend, the next his ex, and just hours ago she sounded set on just keeping her options open—

"Our feelings. Our attraction. Our potential—oh, you know, whatever we have," Mary said with a wave of her hand. "And that's not the point, anyway!"

"What *is* the point?"

"That just because Robbie's more responsible than he used to be doesn't mean he's ready for Vegas," Mary replied. "And I can't believe Mom and Dad can't figure that out."

Matt sighed. "What am I supposed to do about it?"

"Be a big brother for once! Act responsibly."

"What?" Matt cried, sitting up. "I *am* responsible. And I *am* a big brother."

"Then act like one!" Mary ran her fingers through her long hair. "Look. I'm getting on a plane to New York in one hour. Before I leave this room, I want you to promise me that if you can't talk Robbie out of going, then you'll keep an eye on him."

"But—"

"No buts," Mary insisted. "Just promise, please."

Matt stood up and faced his sister. "Okay, I promise. I'll keep the wild women of Las Vegas away from your precious Robbie"—Matt smiled devilishly—"and keep them for myself."

Mary hugged her brother. "Thank you, Matt. I knew I could count on you."

"Yeah, sure," Matt said.

How hard can it be to watch Robbie? Matt thought. He'd still have time for fun.

Matt said goodbye to his sister, then went to his room to pack. He was almost done when he heard a knock.

Mrs. Camden was standing in the

doorway. "Can I have a word with you, Matt?"

"Sure, Mom." Matt threw a few shirts into the suitcase spread out on the bed.

"I'm not comfortable with this Las Vegas trip," said Mrs. Camden.

Matt smiled. "Don't worry. I already promised Mary that I'd keep my eye on Robbie."

"Well, that's good," Mrs. Camden said, frowning. "But that's not what I'm talking about."

"Come on, Mom. You know I'm the most responsible guy in this family. I won't get into any trouble or—"

"You *are* responsible," Mrs. Camden said, interrupting him. "You're a good, decent, moderately responsible son. That's why I want you to keep an eye on your father."

Matt blinked. "Dad?"

Mrs. Camden sighed. "You know how he is. Your father has this thing about rushing in and rescuing damsels in distress—like that divorced parishioner Serena, who needed counseling. And women like Serena, well, they often have questionable agendas."

Mrs. Camden's hands were now on her hips. "Your father is a warm, giving, trusting man. Unfortunately, that combination of virtues seems to attract needy women."

"Mom," Matt began, "you're being silly. Dad loves you. He just likes to help people."

Mrs. Camden shook her head. "I know he loves me, Matt. And I know he likes to help people. It's just that sometimes he gets so involved, he doesn't see where he might be taken advantage of—"

Matt steadied her. "Okay," he said. "I'll keep an eye on Dad. I promise."

"Gee," said a sarcastic voice from the doorway. "If you don't trust Dad, you should ask Robbie to watch him. *Robbie's* more responsible than Matt!"

Mrs. Camden whirled around. "Ruthie! I trust your father—I just don't trust Vegas."

"Excuse me, Ruthie," interrupted Matt in an annoyed tone. "But what makes you think Robbie is more responsible than I am?"

"About a thousand things," Ruthie replied. "He helps out around the house. He helps me do my homework. He helps

Dad at the church. And he even helps Mom with the chores."

"I help out," Matt said. "Right, Mom?"

Mrs. Camden looked at Ruthie, then at Matt.

"I'm going to stay out of this," she said noncommittally. Then she hugged her son.

"Thanks, Matt," Mrs. Camden said. "You don't know how much I appreciate this."

"You can count on me," Matt replied.

Mrs. Camden said goodbye and wished him luck. When she was gone, Matt turned to Ruthie.

"You *know* I'm responsible," he said.

She nodded. "You've always been responsible in a big brother sort of way. But ever since Mom and Dad invited Robbie to live with us, he's been *super* responsible around here. Maybe it's because he's so grateful to have a home. But whatever the reason"—Ruthie shrugged—"he's just more responsible."

"Great," Matt said, not happy with Ruthie's reply. "If Robbie is so responsible, go tell him all about it. I'm busy."

"Okay," Ruthie said. "Have a great trip. And have fun baby-sitting Dad."

And Robbie, Matt reminded himself.

"I won't be baby-sitting anyone," Matt lied as he chased his little sister away and closed the door behind her. By the time he finished packing, Matt's vision of a trouble-free trip had completely evaporated.

TWO

"What's that noise?" Reverend Camden asked, waking with a start.

He was sitting on the passenger side of the minivan. Matt was in the driver's seat.

"I think we have a flat tire," Matt said. "I'm looking for a place to pull over."

"There!" Robbie cried from the back-seat, pointing. "A gas station ahead."

In the distance, shimmering in the desert haze, Matt could just make out the sign. The place was a general rest stop with a small motel, and a restaurant, too.

He steered the limping minivan toward the gas station's crowded parking lot. The restaurant and motel both looked packed with holiday travelers.

Matt climbed out and looked at the tire.

"How bad is it?" asked his father, walking up behind him.

"About as bad as one of Ruthie's flour-and-water pancakes," answered Matt with a sigh. "Flat, flat, flat."

Reverend Camden turned to Robbie. "How far are we from Las Vegas?"

Robbie checked the map in his jacket pocket and frowned. "About one hundred miles."

"And the tire's definitely shot," Reverend Camden agreed, bending to examine it himself. "Until we change it, we're not going anywhere."

"We have a spare," Matt announced. "Two spares, in fact."

"Good. Let's go see if we can find someone to do the work," Reverend Camden said, heading off to the repair shop.

"Sorry," the service station manager told them a few minutes later. "I got three cars needing major repairs. It's a holiday and these drivers are all stranded. I don't have time to change a tire. Maybe in a few hours."

"We understand," Reverend Camden

replied. "We'll change it ourselves. It will just take the guys a little longer."

"I'll get right on it," Matt cried over his shoulder as he rushed off.

Robbie chased after him. "No. *I'll* get right on it."

"Both of you get right on it," Reverend Camden called after them. "I'm going to give Annie a call."

Matt unloaded the spare tire while Robbie dug out the tools. They jacked up the van and pulled the hubcap off. Then Matt went to work on the lug nuts. All of them came off but one. It seemed to be stuck in place.

"I guess it's rusty," Matt said. He rubbed his hands together and got a better grip on the wrench.

"You're stripping the nut," Robbie cautioned him.

Matt looked up. "I know," he said. "I'll be careful."

He tried again. The nut wouldn't budge.

Matt dropped the wrench. It bounced off the concrete with a sharp clang.

"It's no use," he groaned. "The thing is stuck and I just can't get it loose. The wrench is stripping the nut really badly."

"Let a real man try," Robbie said, shouldering Matt aside.

Matt watched as Robbie struggled for several minutes.

"It's hopeless," Robbie sighed, wiping his brow.

"I told you," Matt gloated.

"Let's go find your father," Robbie said. "He'll know what to do."

But before they could go, their eyes were drawn to an unlikely sight—a vision that seemed to appear like a ghostly mirage in the distance.

It was Elvis! Or, whoever he was, he sure looked like Elvis. The man was dressed in a white rhinestone-studded jumpsuit that sparkled in the blazing sun. He had dark sideburns and swept-back hair with a lock dangling over his forehead. His thin lips were curled in a distinctive sneer and dark sunglasses shaded his eyes.

"Is that—"

"In the flesh," Matt replied.

The man sauntered down the shimmering highway, then crossed the median strip. To the guys' surprise, Elvis approached them.

"Havin' a car problem there, boys?" he said with a drawl.

Matt shifted uncomfortably. Robbie smiled at the man. "Hey," he said, shaking Elvis's hand. "I'm Robbie. This is Matt."

"Hey yourself," Elvis replied, eyeing Robbie from behind his shades. Then the stranger bent low and examined the tire. The guys could hear the rhinestones on his jumpsuit click against the pavement.

Elvis stood up again. "I used to have a whole stable full of cars. Kept them all at my home in Memphis—a place called Graceland. Maybe you heard of it?"

Matt and Robbie both nodded nervously. They didn't know what to make of this guy. Was he just an impostor acting in character—or plain crazy?

"I had this problem before, too," Elvis continued. "Especially with my pink Caddy convertible. Cadillacs are nice cars. Expensive, too. You'd think they would come with better wheel bolts." Elvis smiled. "It's the simple things that always make a difference."

"I think I'm gonna go find Dad," Matt said.

"Ahhh, me too," Robbie said. "That is,

I'm going to help him find *his* dad. It was nice to meet you, Mr.—"

"Elvis," the man replied. "Just call me Elvis."

When they were far enough away, Robbie faced Matt. "That was weird."

"Yeah," Matt said. They both fought the urge to look over their shoulders.

"Still, there's something familiar about that guy," Matt said thoughtfully.

"Duh," Robbie replied. "He's Elvis!"

"Not that," Matt hissed, searching his memory. "It's something else . . . I mean, he's somebody else."

Robbie shrugged. "Bob Dylan?"

The boys were diverted from their search for Reverend Camden by the snack bar. While they were waiting in line for food, Reverend Camden returned to the parking lot.

"Excuse me, but I don't think this is your car," Reverend Camden said.

The man leaning against the minivan smiled. The rhinestones on his jumpsuit shimmered in the glare of the desert sun.

"Nope," Elvis replied. "This car belongs to two young men named Robbie and

Matt. They should be back in a minute."

Reverend Camden looked down. The flat tire was off and the spare was in place. The jack and wrench were stacked neatly on top of the flat, waiting to be loaded into the minivan.

"Reverend Camden, you got the tire fixed!" Robbie cried. He and Matt were both carrying snacks from the refreshment area.

"Not me," Reverend Camden replied. "I think it was this man here."

"Elvis," the man said, shaking Reverend Camden's hand.

"Well . . . Elvis," Reverend Camden replied. "We really appreciate your help. Is there anything we can do for you?"

Elvis's lip curled into his trademark smile. "Point me at a ride to Las Vegas and I'll say good night."

"You don't have a car?" Matt asked, studying the man's features carefully.

"I used to have a lot of them," Elvis replied with an indifferent shrug. "Now I rely on the kindness of strangers to get from place to place. Funny thing is, I always get where I'm going."

"I guess we could give you a lift," Matt said. Reverend Camden looked surprised, then nodded.

"Sure," he said. "We're going to Las Vegas. Hop in."

Elvis nodded. "Thank you very much."

As Matt climbed behind the wheel, Reverend Camden leaned close to him and whispered, "We're not supposed to pick up hitchhikers."

"I know," Matt whispered back. "But this guy needs help. And there's something about him that's familiar."

Matt paused. He glanced at the stranger's reflection in the rearview mirror. The jet-black hair and pale complexion. The familiar profile. The trademark sneer. It was Elvis. Or was it?

"I feel like I know him, or I've seen him someplace before," Matt said softly.

Reverend Camden chuckled. "You and everybody else."

"My momma used to say that two things will always clear yo head," Elvis announced from the backseat. "A long stretch of highway or a short visit to the chapel. There wasn't a chapel big enough to clear my head—no offense, Reverend—

so I took off on the longest road trip ever."

Robbie smiled. "You just left it all behind."

"That's right," Elvis replied. "I was too old to reenlist in the army. That's another way to see the world. Have you boys ever thought about signing up?"

"Not really," Robbie said.

Matt shook his head. "I'm in college now."

"Well, if college doesn't work out, try the army," Elvis said with a smile. "I met my wife while I was in the army, you know."

"Elvis," Reverend Camden said, "what are you going to do when you get to Las Vegas? Do you have a job lined up? A place to stay?"

Elvis smiled. "Well, I—"

Just then, an old Elvis tune came on the radio. "Hey, there, Reverend Camden sir, could you please turn that radio up some?"

Reverend Camden turned the dial. The music filled the minivan. As the second verse kicked in, Elvis began to sing along with the voice on the radio.

Suddenly Matt felt a shiver run down

his spine. It was like he was listening to a stereo recording—the voice over the radio and the man singing in the car sounded identical.

When the song ended, Reverend Camden turned the radio off.

"You have a beautiful singing voice," he said.

Elvis smiled. "It's great to know I never lost it. My momma always said my voice was my gift from on high."

The minivan swerved a little. Reverend Camden looked hard at Matt.

"Watch the road, Matt," he warned.

"Sorry," Matt apologized. But he couldn't stop watching the man in his rearview mirror.

Where have I seen him before? Matt wondered.

"Look at that!" Elvis exclaimed. "Bigger and brighter than ever before. A jewel in the desert."

In the distance, the glowing lights of Las Vegas twinkled in the setting sun.

THREE

"Whoa!" Robbie cried, eyes wide.

"Is that—" Matt gulped. He watched in awe as fire spewed from the top of a gigantic water fountain.

"Yep," Robbie said. "It's a real live volcano. In the middle of Main Street."

Matt stepped on the brakes as the traffic slowed to a crawl. A crowd gathered on the sidewalk to watch the fiery display.

"Look!" Matt cried, pointing to a huge black shape in the distance. "A pyramid!"

"There's a medieval castle!" Robbie said.

"Over there. It's a pirate ship. A real pirate ship," Matt said excitedly.

"Maybe I should drive," Reverend

Camden suggested nervously. "You both seem distracted."

"It's amazing," Matt gushed. "I never imagined Las Vegas was so big. And so bright. Look at all those lights."

"Yeah," Robbie said. "Now I know why Elvis wears sunglasses all the time."

Elvis chuckled. "The town's sure changed a lot since I was here last. But I'll bet they still remember the King."

"Turn here," Robbie said, glancing at the map. "The Showbiz Hotel is off to the right."

Matt swerved and entered a new flow of traffic. A few minutes later, the Showbiz Hotel loomed in the distance.

"Whoa!" Robbie cried once again.

"Well, it's not that big, really," Matt said, trying to sound unimpressed and failing. They parked as close as they could get to the entrance and got out. They crossed the sun-washed parking lot and entered the luxurious crystal and neon-lit interior.

Reverend Camden whistled. "We could fit just about every house on our block inside this place!"

"Yeah," Robbie replied. "And this is just the lobby."

"Come on, guys, you're embarrassing me," Matt said. "Let's not act like country bumpkins."

"Son," Reverend Camden said, "if you really want to look sophisticated, then you might try closing your mouth. You're gawking."

Matt snapped his jaws shut. But he still gawked. He had never imagined a place as big and bright and loud as the Showbiz Hotel could even exist. It took them ten minutes just to walk from the car to the front desk.

"The tickets are under my name," Robbie said. "I guess I should register."

"I'll go, too," said Reverend Camden. They left Matt behind with the luggage, and with Elvis.

"This town has sure changed a lot since my heyday," Elvis said.

"Really?" Matt replied. "And when was that?"

Elvis smiled his trademark half-smile, half-sneer. "In the golden age of rock 'n' roll, when I was King."

Matt's gaze drifted to a cluster of pretty young women gathered around the valet parking area. They were looking back, but not at him. The girls were admiring Elvis.

"This town is famous for its ladies," said Elvis, smiling at them.

Matt reddened. Elvis peeked at him over his shades. "Not popular with the ladies?"

"S-sure," Matt stammered. "Sure I am. I'm popular."

"I was asking because you seemed a little shy."

"Shy?" Matt said, too quickly. "There's nothing shy about me."

"Then why don't you saunter over there and introduce yourself to one of those fine ladies?"

Matt glanced at the women, then looked at Elvis. "Because I have other plans."

Elvis chuckled. "You *are* shy."

"Hey, they're not looking at me," Matt said. "They're looking at you. You're the King."

"Any man can be the King," Elvis replied. "It's in the hips."

Elvis demonstrated. He shimmied to a

riff of imaginary music. Matt flushed. The ladies watched and seemed quite impressed.

"Learn to hop and the ladies will flock," Elvis told him.

"I can dance," Matt said.

"Show me."

"What?"

"Show me your moves."

Matt stared at Elvis. "I'm not gonna dance here. There's no music."

Elvis smiled. "There's always music. You just have to learn to hear it."

Robbie returned before Matt could reply.

"I got the room," he announced. "A suite with plenty enough space for everyone."

"Where's Dad?"

Robbie shrugged. "The last time I saw him, he was talking to some girl over there. She was pretty, too."

Matt turned to the direction Robbie was pointing. A very attractive young woman in a short leather skirt was talking to his father.

"Oh no," Matt groaned. "Why didn't you stop him?"

Robbie looked up. "Stop him from what? Having a conversation?"

"Stay here with Elvis," Matt cried. "I have to break this up."

Matt rushed to his father. "Ah . . . Dad. We've got the room," he announced, trying to position himself between his father and the young woman. "We can go upstairs now, and you can call Mom."

The woman blinked. Then she smiled at Reverend Camden. "Well, thank you for your help," she said, then walked away.

Reverend Camden turned to Matt. "That was rude."

"Help!" Matt cried. "Help! What kind of help?"

Reverend Camden stared at Matt. "She had a rental car," he replied. "I gave her instructions on how to get to Boulder Dam. We just passed it, so I knew the way."

"Oh," Matt said, reddening. "Boulder Dam. She . . . she just wanted to see . . . Boulder Dam."

Reverend Camden nodded.

"Great!" Matt said, clapping his hands. "Shall we go to our room?"

"Where's Robbie?" Reverend Camden asked.

"I left him over there with Elvis."

"I see Robbie," Reverend Camden said. "But I don't see Elvis."

Matt turned. His father was right.

Elvis had left the building.

Matt pushed his way through the crowd and confronted Robbie.

"What's the matter with you?" he cried. "I left you alone for one minute and you let Elvis get away."

"Get away?" said Robbie. "I didn't know he was our prisoner. Anyway, he's got to be around here somewhere."

"We've got to find him," Matt said as he scanned the room.

"Why do we have to find him? He's a fake."

"Shut up and look for Elvis," Matt snapped, his tone sharper than normal. He didn't see Robbie's angry expression. His eyes were still searching the lobby.

"Shut up?" Robbie shot back. "I warned you not to act like my chaperon on this trip. And don't tell me to shut up."

Matt ignored Robbie and rushed over to the front desk.

"Excuse me," he said, interrupting a conversation. "Have you seen a guy who looks like Elvis walking around here?"

The receptionist shot Matt a sour look.

"This is Las Vegas, son," he said. "Are you asking me how many Elvis sightings I had today, or just in the last hour?"

Reverend Camden and Robbie caught up with him.

"What's the matter with you, Matt?" Reverend Camden demanded.

"Yeah, what's your problem?" Robbie challenged. He was still angry.

"We've got to find that guy," Matt replied. "I *know* him. I'm sure of it."

"Calm down, Matt," Reverend Camden said. "He's got to be around here somewhere."

"He'd still be here if Robbie acted more responsibly."

"Hold on, Matt," Reverend Camden warned.

"Are you always this rude?" Robbie said. "Do you act like this at work, too? If you do, it's a wonder you can still hold a job!"

Matt's eyes went wide. "Work! That's it! It was at the hospital!"

Robbie and Reverend Camden were confused. Matt was about to explain when he suddenly spied Elvis. The man was at the other end of the lobby.

Matt broke away from his father and ran toward Elvis.

"Don't leave! Don't leave!" Matt cried, stumbling through the crowd that packed the sumptuous lobby.

Matt had almost pushed his way through the mob when Elvis made a break for the door.

"Wait!" Matt cried. "Don't go! Dr. Mitchell! Please don't go."

Elvis's back was to Matt when he called out the name, but the man in the jumpsuit paused.

"Stop, Dr. Mitchell. Let's talk!" Matt cried.

But Elvis hurried out the door. He didn't even turn around.

An elevator opened and a bunch of people poured into the lobby, blocking Matt's way. He watched helplessly as the white jumpsuit faded into the desert twilight.

FOUR

"And you're absolutely certain that our Elvis is really this Dr. Mitchell guy?" Reverend Camden asked.

Matt nodded. "I'm positive. It just took me a long time to recognize him because he looks so different in an Elvis costume. I remember him wearing surgical scrubs. His new look kind of threw me off."

They were sitting together in Robbie's spacious suite at the Showbiz Hotel. Outside the big picture window, the neon lights of the city brilliantly illuminated the arid night.

Father and son were alone. Robbie was still annoyed with Matt, and Reverend Camden sent him off to find his friend

Tony Carr. He thought that would be best. Reverend Camden sensed some tension between Matt and Robbie and figured they needed some space. For some reason, the rivalry that always simmered below the surface had heated up in recent days.

"Why have you never mentioned this Dr. Mitchell before?" Reverend Camden asked.

"He was only at Glenoak for a few days, and that was months ago," Matt explained. "Right after I began working at the hospital. I don't know what he was doing there, just that Dr. Mitchell was a specialist of some sort. Pediatrics. Heart surgery. Something."

Reverend Camden searched his memory.

"You know," he said at last. "I remember when that little seven-year-old girl needed special surgery, and Father Gates—the hospital chaplain—arranged for her to have free treatment. That was heart surgery, wasn't it?"

"That's right!" Matt cried, jumping to his feet. "I remember now! Dr. Mitchell came to Glenoak because he was one of the few doctors in the world who could perform that particular operation. That's when I met him."

"Are you sure it was Dr. Mitchell in the car with us today?" Reverend Camden said. "Absolutely, positively certain?"

"I am," Matt declared. "One day I cornered Dr. Mitchell in the break room. Told him I wanted to be a doctor. He was nice. Told me about his family. How hard he worked to get his medical degree. We talked for a long time."

Reverend Camden shrugged. "Well, if he really is this eminent pediatric heart surgeon, then what is Dr. Mitchell doing wandering around the deserts of Nevada pretending to be Elvis?"

"I don't know," Matt said. "But I intend to find out. I'm going to call the hospital. Maybe someone in the main office will know about Dr. Mitchell."

"Matt, you know no one at the hospital can give out personal information about Dr. Mitchell. Besides, it's New Year's Eve, and I'm sure they're short-staffed as it is," Reverend Camden reminded him.

Matt's shoulders sagged. His dad was right. But he still felt responsible for losing Elvis. Matt suspected that Dr. Mitchell was in some kind of trouble. Matt didn't know why he felt that way, but he did.

I shouldn't have called out his name, Matt thought. *It scared him off, I'm sure of it.*

"Come on," Reverend Camden said. "There's nothing we can do now. Let's go find Robbie. You owe him an apology, or at least an explanation."

Matt shook his head. "I don't want to tell him anything about Dr. Mitchell. Not until I'm certain."

"Fine," Reverend Camden said, leading him to the door. "Then all you have to do is apologize."

"Apologize!"

Reverend Camden stopped and nodded. "Apologize for telling Robbie to shut up."

Matt's shoulders sagged. It was turning out to be an awful vacation.

They found Robbie on the gigantic stage of the Showbiz Auditorium. The room was empty except for the band, three backup singers, and some technicians who were setting up equipment and performing sound checks.

An electrician showed them how to get

backstage. Matt and Reverend Camden walked through a long hall and came out behind the curtain on the main stage.

"Reverend Camden, over here!" Robbie called, ignoring Matt.

Reverend Camden smiled and approached a group of six young men dressed in identical lime green suits. The backup singers, all wearing lime green miniskirts, smiled a greeting. They had beehive hairdos, pink lipstick, and long eyelashes.

"This is my friend Tony Carr," Robbie said, introducing Reverend Camden to a lanky youth with frizzy red hair and freckles. "Tony is the lead guitar player of this group."

They shook hands.

"Welcome to our first dress rehearsal," Tony said with a grin. "These are the Lime-lighters."

Tony turned and faced the girls. "Here's our backup singers, Megan, Tiffany, and Amber."

The girls giggled and waved.

Tony pointed to a short man with glasses sitting behind the drum set.

"That's Tim Luna on the skins." The man rose and bowed.

"This is Alex Tribe, our sax player. Rex Ingram our bass guitarist. Terry Rhythm is on keyboards." The three shook hands with Matt and Reverend Camden.

Tony turned and pointed to the far end of the stage. "That guy over there clutching his stomach is Rod Dermain, our lead singer. Rod does a fair impression of Mick Jagger, a good version of Buddy Holly, and an absolutely fabulous Elvis."

The man called Rod looked up. His face was sweaty, his eyes glassy and feverish. He nodded at Reverend Camden and then hunched back over.

"He looks sick," Reverend Camden said. "Is he okay?"

Tony shrugged. "Just nerves, I guess. Stage fright. I'm sure he'll be fine by show time."

While Reverend Camden and Tony talked, Matt sidled up to Robbie.

"Hey," Matt said.

"Hey," Robbie replied.

"Look, I'm—"

"Don't apologize," Robbie interrupted.

"You don't have to. I guess I should have been more responsible and not let Elvis get away. Maybe that guy needed help. Maybe I messed up."

Matt shook his head. "No, it was my fault, and I want to apologize. So I'm sorry for telling you to shut up. I'll never do it again."

Robbie chuckled. "I never thought I'd live to hear that."

"What?"

"You apologizing to me. It's kind of amazing—admit it."

Matt thought about it and nodded. "It is, isn't it?" he said.

"Well," Reverend Camden announced, throwing his arms over Matt's and Robbie's shoulders, "now that that's settled, I'm going to take off."

He glanced at his watch. "I'm heading back to the room to make a phone call."

Reverend Camden turned to the band. "Good luck tonight. I guess I'll see you later, at the show."

Matt watched his father depart, wondering if he should go with him. He'd promised his mom he'd keep an eye on Dad.

But he also promised Mary he'd keep an eye on Robbie. Even now, one of the backup singers was flirting with Robbie, who pretended to ignore her.

Matt thought about his options and, knowing that both his father and Robbie were trustworthy, he decided on a third course of action. He decided to look around the hotel for any sign of Elvis.

He's probably halfway to Utah by now, Matt told himself. But he still had to try. He felt responsible for the man, even if he didn't really understand what was going on inside Dr. Mitchell's head—if that was Dr. Mitchell.

"I'll be back in a half hour or so," Matt told Robbie. "See you then."

FIVE

Matt wandered around the gigantic hotel for forty-five minutes. He circled the swimming pool, visited the luxury spa, the patio restaurant, even the parking lot. Matt spotted a few Elvis impersonators, but not Dr. Mitchell.

He began to have doubts.

Maybe I'm totally crazy, Matt thought. *Maybe I was wrong about Elvis. Maybe we gave a ride to some performer who gets his kicks out of creating Elvis sightings.*

Matt sat down near a fountain and rubbed his eyes.

This can't go on, he thought miserably. *I'm driving myself crazy over this. Even if Elvis really is Dr. Mitchell, what's that got to do with me? It's not my responsibility, is it?*

He shook his head to clear it.

I have to be wrong, Matt told himself at last. *The Elvis we picked up was just some nutty performer. Dr. Mitchell is probably in an operating room right now, saving someone's life. I should save* my *life—or at least my vacation—and forget about all this nuttiness once and for all.*

Suddenly Matt felt about a thousand pounds lighter, like a great weight had been lifted off his shoulders.

I should go find Robbie and Dad. We should all get a bite to eat before the big show tonight. Then we should watch the band, sing and dance, and have a great New Year's Eve.

Matt felt much better as he walked up to the main entrance of the Showbiz Hotel. As he passed through the revolving doors, the unexpected chill from the air-conditioning made Matt shiver—or was it the sight of the paramedics clustered around a man lying on the ground?

Matt cornered a bellhop. "What's going on?"

"Scariest thing," the bellhop replied. "This old guy was standing there, waiting to check in, when suddenly he grabbed his chest and collapsed."

"Heart attack?" Matt asked.

The bellhop nodded. "That'd be my guess. But I'm no doctor. Good thing Elvis was here."

The hairs on the back of Matt's neck prickled. "Elvis?"

"Yeah," said the bellhop. "I'm not kidding. It was Elvis. As I was dialing 911, this guy in an Elvis costume rushed over and began giving the old guy CPR."

"You're sure he was wearing an Elvis costume?"

"Positive," the bellhop said. "I know the King when I see him. White rhinestone-studded jumpsuit. Sideburns. Sneer. Sunglasses." The bellhop shrugged. "It was Elvis."

"Thanks," Matt said, numb with shock. He glanced over at the paramedics. They were feeding the old man oxygen. He seemed alert and was even talking.

Matt drifted closer and noticed a distraught woman, obviously the old man's wife. Matt listened to her conversation with one of the paramedics.

"Your husband will be fine, ma'am,"

the medic said. "That guy who administered CPR, whoever he was, knew his stuff. He probably saved your husband's life."

"It was Elvis!" the woman cried. "Elvis saved my Sidney!"

Matt shook his head. There was no doubt about it now. *It was Dr. Mitchell! It had to be!*

He had to find his father!

Matt hurried to the elevators. The ride up to the tenth floor seemed to take forever. When Matt finally reached the hotel room, it was empty. A pen and a crumpled-up piece of paper were lying on the desk near the telephone. It looked like someone had been writing down notes or something.

No time for that now, Matt decided. *I have to find Dad.*

Matt finally located his father back at the Showbiz Auditorium. Reverend Camden was with Robbie. They were both standing over a male band member, who was lying on the ground with a rolled-up towel under his head.

Reverend Camden held a cold compress to the young man's forehead.

"Relax, Rod," Reverend Camden said

in a soothing voice. "We're going to get you to a doctor as soon as the ambulance arrives."

"What's going on?" Matt asked.

Reverend Camden looked up. "I was looking for you, Matt."

"I was looking for you, too. Dad, I—"

Reverend Camden shook his head. "Not now. We have an emergency situation here, so whatever it is, it will have to wait."

He looked down at Rod, who moaned in pain.

"It seems that Rod might have appendicitis," Reverend Camden said. "We're waiting for the paramedics."

Rod was doubled up and clutching his belly. One of the backup singers sobbed and dabbed away a tear.

Paramedics appeared, pushing a wheeled stretcher onto the stage. As they gingerly lifted Rod onto the gurney, Matt could hear excited voices arguing. In the corner, Tony raged to the other band members.

"We're ruined!" he cried. "How can the show go on without a lead singer?"

Matt felt a tap on his shoulder. "I'm going to the hospital with Rod," Reverend

Camden told him. "When I get back, we'll have that talk."

Matt grabbed his arm. "Don't go yet—"

"Reverend," a paramedic called. "If you're coming, get a move on. Our patient is spiking a high fever."

"On my way," Reverend Camden said, following the paramedics to the ambulance outside.

Matt stood in the center of the stage, alone with his thoughts. Things were happening so fast his head was spinning.

"Hey, Matt," Robbie called. "The band's having a sit-down. Want to come?"

Matt shrugged. He wasn't sure what he should do next, so he followed Robbie and the others to the dressing room.

Tony was already addressing his troops. "So we put the girls up front to do the singing, give Alex a sax solo in the first set and Tim a drum solo during the second set, then . . ."

Tony paused and sat back. "Then I guess that takes care of the first two-thirds of the show. But we still have to figure out what to do about the climax. We need a lead singer for our closing number, if nothing else."

Tim adjusted his glasses. "Not necessarily," he said. As he spoke, Tim tossed his drumsticks into the air and caught them.

"What do you mean?" Tony asked.

"I mean we recorded the rehearsal show yesterday," Tim replied. "Why not use the tape?"

Tony got excited. "Hey! That's right!"

Robbie scratched his head. "So you recorded it? So what?"

"Don't you get it!" Tony cried. "We can use the recording Rod made yesterday for the climax. We don't need a singer."

"What?" Alex said, unconvinced. "You're going to ask the audience to stop everything and listen to a *recording*? Are you nuts?"

"No, he's right!" Terry grinned. "The big acts do it all the time, especially on television."

"Sure," Tony continued. "We play the recording, and get somebody out there in costume to lip-synch the words, do the dance, whatever it takes to make the audience think they're really seeing something!"

"Somebody to lip-synch?" Alex said. "Like who?"

The Limelighters exchanged glances, then studied Robbie.

"Too short," Tony said, shaking his head.

"Yeah," Megan added. "He'd never fit into Rod's costume."

"What about him?"

Matt looked up. He hadn't been paying much attention to the band's discussion. He was mired in his own thoughts about the mysterious Dr. Mitchell. Now everyone in the room was staring at him. And Robbie was chuckling. Matt knew it couldn't be good.

"What?" Matt said.

"Ever wanted to be a rock 'n' roll star?" Tim chuckled.

"Oh no," Matt said. "Not me. You don't want me to perform tonight. It would be a disaster."

"That's true," Robbie said. "I've seen Matt dance."

"I think he'd be perfect," Tiffany gushed. "He's the same height as Rod, but with a much dreamier face. I'll bet the costume would fit him like a glove."

"Hey, wait a minute!" Matt cried as the band circled him.

Tony grabbed Matt's shoulders. "You would be doing us a big favor, maybe saving our lives. And all you have to do is put on a costume. Lip-synch a song. Dance around. I mean, how hard is *that*?"

Matt tried to refuse, but the band members wouldn't take no for an answer.

"Come on," Tim begged. "You'd save the Limelighters. And everyone's big night out. It's New Year's Eve. The show must go on."

"Yeah," Amber gushed. "And I know you'd be great. You're so cute. The women will love you."

"I don't know," Matt said, warming to the idea now.

Tim shook his head. "If he can't do it—"

"Well, I think he'd be great!" Tony declared. He turned to Megan.

"Go get Rod's costume out of his dressing room. Let's see how Matt looks in it."

"Come on," Matt pleaded. "This is silly."

Robbie sat back in his chair and laughed. Before Matt could react, Amber and Tiffany dragged him out of his chair and began fussing with his hair.

"He'll be perfect," Amber gushed.

"I'm sure the costume will fit," said Tiffany, squeezing his arm. "And look at those muscles."

"Come on," Matt said. Then he smiled at Tiffany. "Do you really think I have muscles?"

"Here's the costume!" Megan cried. She carried a wardrobe bag over her shoulder.

"Come on, guys," Matt continued. "I can't sing. I can't dance. I probably don't even know the song."

Tony chuckled. "Everybody knows the song. It's 'Love Me Tender.'"

Matt paled. Robbie's mouth snapped shut. Matt turned around just as the girls pulled the garment out of the protective bag.

Smiling, Megan held up a gleaming white '70s-style jumpsuit, complete with high collar and hundreds of glittering rhinestones.

"Say it isn't so," Matt whispered.

Robbie laughed out loud. "Oh, this is *too* good!" he cried.

Tony looked at Matt, then at Robbie. He knew he was missing something.

"What's the matter?" Tony demanded.

No one replied. Matt was in shock, and Robbie was laughing too hard.

"It's not funny. It's a Showbiz Hotel tradition," Tony explained. "The New Year's Eve show always ends with an Elvis song."

A few minutes later, Robbie was helping Matt change into the jumpsuit.

SIX

"I can't believe you roped me into this!" Matt exclaimed.

Robbie adjusted Matt's collar, then handed him a pair of sunglasses. "I didn't rope you into anything," he replied. "You volunteered."

"I was drafted!" Matt cried. "Against my will, too."

"Drafted or not, you're doing the right thing. You wanted Elvis, and you got him."

Robbie perched the sunglasses on the end of Matt's nose. Matt reached up and adjusted them. Suddenly he was blind. He almost tripped over Tiffany, who was buffing his platform shoes to a brilliant shine.

"I can't see a thing," Matt complained. "And this outfit is hot, uncomfortable, and heavy. These rhinestones must weigh a ton. And I can hardly stand in these shoes. How am I supposed to dance?"

"Stop whining," Robbie said. "You sound like Ruthie."

Amber fussed with Matt's hair, adding some mousse that slicked it down and made it shine. She put her fingers to her lips and moistened them. Then she took a strand of Matt's hair and curled it over his forehead.

When she stepped back, the room became very quiet. Robbie whistled.

"I can't believe it," Tiffany gushed.

"It's incredible," Amber declared.

"If I hadn't seen it, I wouldn't have believed it," Robbie said.

"This is ridiculous," Matt said with a sigh.

Then he stepped up to the full-length mirror and gazed at his reflection. Matt gasped, too.

"I really do look like Elvis!" he cried in amazement.

"You surely do," Amber said.

Matt preened and mugged for the

mirror. He strutted back and forth, then struck a theatrical pose. He tried to twirl around, but lost his footing on the platform shoes and barely caught himself. Matt reddened and looked in the mirror again.

I am the King!

"You look marvelous," Tony said as he entered the room. "The costume fits you perfectly."

"Yeah," Matt said, nodding. "I guess clothes do make the man."

Robbie looked doubtful. "Clothes might make the man, but there's only one King. I hope Matt can cut it."

Tony glanced at his watch. "Show time is in two hours," he announced. "Let's teach Matt the routine, and try to get in a rehearsal before the show actually begins."

Robbie stepped back and crossed his arms.

"This should be *good*," he said with a chuckle.

During the next two hours, Matt tried his hardest to learn the King's moves. But from the looks on the faces of the backup singers, the tune on their minds was *try, try, again!*

"I didn't think it was possible for some- one to have more than two left feet," Amber whispered. Megan nodded. So did Tiffany. The three singers were sitting in the third row of the auditorium's seats, watching Matt stumble through the routine.

"It's kind of sad," Megan said. "He's so cute otherwise."

"But about as graceful as a rhino," said Amber.

"Maybe I can file for unemployment," Megan said with a groan.

"No! No!" Tony cried, cutting off the music. "You take two steps forward, three back, then sway your hips and *then* twirl around. Come on, Matt. Try it again."

Matt attempted to perform the simple dance routine. The two steps forward went fine, so did the three steps back. He swayed his hips in an Elvis fashion, but when he twirled, Matt stumbled over a microphone cord.

"Whoa!"

Matt fell to the stage floor with a loud thump. Rhinestones popped off the cos- tume and bounced around him.

"Are you all right?" Robbie called from backstage. Matt could hear the amusement in his voice.

"I'm fine," Matt replied. He was sprawled on his back and blinking against the glare of the bright lights.

Tony kicked aside a few rhinestones and helped Matt to his feet. Matt swayed unsteadily on the high platform shoes.

"Fall a few more times, and the costume will be a lot lighter," Tony said, kicking rhinestones into the orchestra pit.

"I'm sorry. I didn't mean to ruin the costume," Matt said, blushing.

"Don't worry. Everything will be fine. I'm sure you'll get the hang of it," Tony lied.

"Maybe Rod is feeling better," Tim said from behind the drum set.

Alex snapped his cell phone shut and shook his head. "That won't happen. I just talked to Reverend Camden over at Las Vegas General Hospital. Rod is in surgery right now. It was appendicitis. He almost bought the big ticket."

"Did my father say when he was coming back here?" Matt asked.

Alex nodded. "He said he was going to stay at the hospital until he knows Rod is okay. He hoped to get back before the show starts, but . . ." Alex shrugged.

"Great," Matt groaned. He had been hoping to be rescued at the last minute. Now that hope was gone.

"Get back to your places, everyone," Tony called, clapping his hands. "Let's try it again from the top. One. Two. Th—"

Crash!

Matt hit the floor again. More rhinestones bounced off the stage and rolled into the corner.

"It's these shoes!" Matt cried, rubbing his knee. "These platform heels are so high nobody could walk in them."

The backup singers giggled from the audience.

"Hey," Amber called. "We walk in high heels all the time."

"Yeah, Matt," Robbie said. "If a girl can do it, why can't you?"

Matt shot Robbie a look that made the others back away.

"Somebody please help him up," Tony said miserably. "Let's try and take it from the top—yet again."

* * *

Show time came all too quickly. Matt watched from the wings of the stage as the Limelighters rocked the house. During a short intermission, the band blew into the dressing room for a breather.

Matt followed them. His big number was coming up soon, and he felt his stomach turning for the third time since the show began. He wanted to return to the rest room, but instead dropped to the long leather couch.

"What a crowd!" Amber gushed. "There's not an empty seat in the house!"

"And we've got the audience in the palm of our hands," Alex said, nodding. "Did you see them stand up and cheer my saxophone solo?"

Tim twirled his drumsticks. "My drum solo is next and I am so ready!"

Tony turned to Matt. "Are you holding up okay?"

Matt raised his head from between his knees and nodded. He was pale and nervous and looked like he was about to faint.

"Maybe if you throw up," Tony suggested. "John Lennon barfed before he went on stage. Said it relieved his stage fright."

Robbie rubbed Matt's shoulders. "He already did that."

"Twice," Matt groaned.

There was a knock on the dressing room door. "Two minutes!" cried a voice from outside.

The band rushed to the stage. Amber and Tiffany paused at the mirror to touch up their faces.

"Let's go! Let's go, people!" Tony cried, clapping his hands. When the dressing room was quiet, he bent low and whispered to Robbie.

"Bring him up in about ten minutes," he said. "You know the cue. I'll announce the King's arrival, then Matt comes out—"

"And falls on his face," Robbie whispered back.

"I heard that," Matt muttered from between his knees.

Tony patted Matt on the back.

"Take deep breaths. The show will be over in no time."

Then he was gone.

Matt raised his head and looked at Robbie.

"I don't think I can do this," he moaned. "My hands are shaking. My knees are weak. And I can't even walk in these shoes."

Robbie steadied Matt.

"Look," he said. "These people are counting on you. I'm counting on you. You have to do this. You promised."

"I was roped into it," Matt shot back.

"No," Robbie corrected him. "You volunteered. You volunteered because my friends were in a jam and you agreed to help them out. You're a good person and it's the responsible thing to do."

"That's me," Matt said. "Mr. Responsibility."

"That's right," Robbie said. "You *are* responsible. And it *is* the right thing to do."

Robbie paused. "And by the way, I owe you some thanks. Thanks for helping out my friends. Thanks for helping me out, too."

Matt looked at Robbie, puzzled.

"I know it's hard," Robbie continued. "You were the big brother of the Camden family, and suddenly I show up and steal your place—"

"You didn't steal my place," Matt said.

"Maybe not," Robbie replied. "But I'm sure it feels like that to you, at least part of the time."

Matt said nothing because Robbie was right. It *did* feel like that sometimes. Maybe that was why Robbie seemed to get under his skin so much.

"I love your family," Robbie continued. "I love my place in it. But if you are uncomfortable, then I will find another place to live. I don't want to steal your family, Matt."

Matt sat up.

"Robbie, you aren't stealing my family. Love is boundless. My family has a big heart. Big enough to fit both you and me."

Robbie smiled. "That means a lot," he said.

Suddenly there was a sharp knock on the dressing room door.

"Elvis is up next," a voice said.

Matt's stomach lurched again. He wanted to run to the rest room again—and then run as far away as he could. Instead, Matt took a deep breath and stood up. He wobbled on his platform shoes as he walked to the door.

"Come on, let's go," Matt said to Robbie. "The show must go on. And I need someone to help me make it onto the stage. I think I can dance in these shoes, but I know I can't walk."

"I'd say break a leg, but you probably will," Robbie replied. "So I'll just wish you luck."

Matt leaned on Robbie's shoulder. Together, they headed for the stage and Matt's rock 'n' roll debut.

SEVEN

Matt could feel his heart pounding in his chest. He felt dizzy, and scared, and excited all at once. Most of all, he just wanted out of there. But flight wasn't an option. He said he'd perform, and that's what he was going to do. Keeping a promise was the responsible thing to do.

Tim Luna's arms were a blur as he finished his drum solo. The beat was contagious. The crowd was on its feet, dancing and swaying to the music.

A stagehand sidled up to Matt. "You're up next," he said.

Matt's knees got so weak he wobbled on his shoes.

"Whoa," Robbie said, trying to steady him.

Tim beat a wild tattoo on the drums, then finished his solo with a thunderous flourish. The crowd went crazy. They jumped to their feet and clapped until the whole arena shook.

Tim stood up, adjusted his glasses, and bowed.

"Thank you, thank you," Tony said as he moved to the center of the stage, his amplified voice booming through the packed auditorium as the applause faded.

"And now we have a real treat," Tony purred. "He's come to Las Vegas all the way from Graceland. . . ."

The crowd began to cheer.

Matt swallowed hard and tried to take a deep breath. The room seemed to spin and he felt like he was about to drown.

Someone handed Matt a microphone. He blinked and stared at it.

"Here he is, ladies and gentlemen," Tony cried. "The King of Rock 'n' Roll himself . . ."

Suddenly Matt felt a hand on his

shoulder. He closed his eyes and prepared to step onto the stage. The hand restrained him. Matt turned, looked up, and his eyes went wide.

"Dr. Mitchell!"

The man smiled. He was wearing a jumpsuit just like Matt's, but on him it looked natural—like he was the King.

"Yes," the man said. "I'm Dr. Mitchell. But for one last time, I'm going to be Elvis. . . ."

"Here he is, folks!" Tony cried. "Elvis!"

Dr. Mitchell plucked the mike out of Matt's hand. Then he looked at Matt and winked.

"I saw your rehearsal earlier today," Dr. Mitchell whispered. "You've really got to work on your dance routine."

Then Dr. Mitchell stepped onto the stage and into the spotlight. The crowd saw him and went wild. As the musical introduction built, Tony rushed backstage and confronted Matt.

"Who is that guy?" he cried.

"It's Elvis."

Tony's eyes went wide. "*The* Elvis?"

Matt smiled. "Let's just say he's a much better Elvis than I will ever be."

Tony looked confused. "What—what should I do?" he stammered.

"Kill the recording and cue that mike," Matt replied. "This Elvis does his own singing."

Tony signaled the stagehand, and the man shut off the recorded song.

While Matt, Robbie, and Tony watched in amazement, Dr. Mitchell launched into a heartfelt, beautifully rendered version of "Love Me Tender." As he sang, the audience could feel the emotion radiating from the singer. Dr. Mitchell's stage presence was truly electrifying. His performance was so polished that Matt almost believed he was the *real* Elvis.

In the middle of the song, someone tapped Matt on the shoulder. He turned to see Reverend Camden. His father had a look of puzzlement on his face. He fingered Matt's costume.

"What is this all about?"

"It's a long story," Matt replied. "But for now, let's just watch the show."

As the song came to an end, Matt turned to his father.

"He really *is* Dr. Mitchell," Matt said.

"I know," Reverend Camden said with

a nod. "His name is Dr. Randall Mitchell, and his family is quite worried about him."

"How do you know?" Matt said, surprised.

"I made a few calls," Reverend Camden confessed.

Matt blinked. "But you said nobody at the hospital office would give us any information."

"I did say that, didn't I?" Reverend Camden said with a grin. "I called Father Gates at home."

"The hospital chaplain, of course!" said Matt.

"Yes," said the reverend. "He told me all about the eminent heart surgeon from New York City who last year volunteered his services to come to Glenoak and operate on a little girl with a life-threatening heart problem."

They watched Dr. Mitchell perform for a moment. He seemed at ease on stage—like he was born to play Elvis. It was hard to believe he was really a physician.

"What's really going on?" Matt said finally. "With Dr. Mitchell, I mean."

Reverend Camden frowned. "About six months ago, Dr. Mitchell's wife and two children were killed in an automobile accident."

"Oh no," Matt gasped. "That's terrible."

"The doctor didn't take the shock of his loss very well," Reverend Camden said. "The funny thing is that some of the stuff Dr. Mitchell told us in the car was true.

"He really did meet his wife in Germany while he was in the army. Only her name wasn't Priscilla, it was Nancy. And they were very much in love.

"After the accident, Dr. Mitchell gave up his practice and fell into a deep depression. One day he simply vanished without a trace," Reverend Camden continued. "I spoke with his sister this afternoon. She's on her way to Las Vegas right now to talk to her brother."

Matt shifted uncomfortably. "Maybe he doesn't want to talk to her."

Reverend Camden nodded. "Maybe not. But I think Dr. Mitchell needs help. And you think so, too, or you wouldn't have driven yourself crazy trying to find him again after you figured out who he really was."

Matt nodded. "You're right. I don't know how I knew, but I sensed Dr. Mitchell was in some kind of trouble."

"He's in pain," Reverend Camden said. "He's trying to run away from that pain by plunging into a fantasy world where he isn't a doctor who's just lost his family— he's Elvis, the King of Rock 'n' Roll."

The song ended and the audience began to cheer. They clapped for five whole minutes. Dr. Mitchell took many bows, but finally moved off the stage.

"You were great! Fabulous!" Tony cried. "The audience wants more. Aren't you going to do an encore?"

Dr. Mitchell shook his head. "No, my days of playing Elvis are over. It's time for me to play doctor again."

Then he faced Matt.

"Maybe you know what happened to me, and maybe you don't," Dr. Mitchell began. "When you called my name out loud this afternoon, it was like an alarm bell went off in my head. I've been crazy with grief for the last six months. I wanted to get away from my world—my life. I wanted to be anyone but Dr. Randall Mitchell. So I became Elvis."

Dr. Mitchell put his hand on Matt's shoulder.

"But I'm through running from my responsibility," he said. "That ends now. Tonight. I'm going to return to my old life, my practice. I still hurt for the things I lost, and that pain will never go away. But neither will I."

Dr. Mitchell smiled. "I have responsibilities. I'm through dodging them."

"That's great, Dr. Mitchell," Reverend Camden said. "I've talked to your sister, Rachel. She's flying out here first thing in the morning to take you back to New York."

Dr. Mitchell nodded. "I guess I owe her an explanation and an apology. I guess I owe a lot of people."

Reverend Camden smiled. "I think you can skip the apology. Rachel is just relieved to hear that you're okay, and she's going to be delighted to see you after all these months."

"I'll have to find a place to stay," Dr. Mitchell said. Then he looked down at the rhinestone-studded jumpsuit he was wearing. "And find some normal clothes."

Reverend Camden put his hand on Dr. Mitchell's shoulder.

"You can stay with us tonight," he

promised. "And in the morning we'll find you some clothes."

"Thank you," Dr. Mitchell said. Then he turned to Matt. "And thank you, son. You saved my sanity. You saved my life."

Matt smiled. "All I did was give you a ride. You did the rest."

Suddenly the arena shook. The crowd was counting down the seconds to the stroke of midnight and the start of a brand-new year.

"Five . . . Four . . . Three . . . Two . . ."

"Happy New Year, Dr. Mitchell," Matt said, shaking his hand. "And welcome home."

Reverend Camden led Dr. Mitchell out of the auditorium.

"I guess you're feeling pretty relieved, huh?" Robbie said. "You didn't have to perform, and now you can take off those crazy duds."

Matt looked over Robbie's shoulder to a group of pretty young women gathering on the edge of the stage. The prettiest girl smiled at him. Matt smiled back. Then all the girls began to giggle.

"You know," Matt said, "I think maybe I'll stay Elvis just a little bit longer."

**HERE'S A SNEAK PEEK
AT THE NEXT 7ᵀᴴ HEAVEN**

WINTER BALL

Coming January 2002!

It was Monday morning at the freshman dorm, and Lucy needed breakfast. She looked in the mirror and shook her head. How could she possibly cross campus looking like she'd just rolled out of bed? She grabbed a ponytail holder and pulled her hair back. But a dozen little strands of blond frayed out from her head to form a frizzy lion's mane.

That looks even worse!

Frustrated, Lucy pulled the band out of her messy hair and grabbed a brush. What was wrong with her these days? Every look she tried was wrong. Wrong, wrong, wrong!

Suddenly she wanted to cry. But why? Was it really so bad to be a freshman at such a cool college?

Maybe the real problem was that she hadn't made any close friends besides her roommate—who had decided to extend her winter vacation for two more weeks. Who was Lucy going to hang out with until she returned?

You look fine the way you are, she counseled herself. *Now go get some food from the cafeteria.*

Lucy pushed open her door and started off down the hallway, where posters, bumper stickers, and pictures were plastered across all the doors. The room across from her had posters of cool bands, and the room to the left was covered with pictures of modern dancers. And then there was the room at the end of the hall. The door was lined with black-and-white photography, taken by the two talented roommates who lived inside.

Lucy's door had a picture of a pink flower on it.

Why did she suddenly feel so boring? How had she been so popular in high school but become utterly invisible in college? All the confidence and security she used to have was gone. She felt like a little seventh grader all over again. Like

Mary Camden's dorky younger sister.

As Lucy reached for the exit door, she heard a stampede behind her. She turned around and saw a whole gang of girls running down the stairs, racing each other.

One girl yelled, "Loser buys breakfast!" The others burst out laughing as they ran right past Lucy. They busted through the hallway door without even noticing her.

She caught the door before it closed again, watching the girls continue their marathon through the quad. She sighed and walked out onto the grassy lawn. When she looked up at the sky, she rolled her eyes: it was dreary and gray. But then again, what else would it be? The weather fit Lucy's mood perfectly. She looked up at the clouds, certain that it was about to rain.

Halfway to the cafeteria, a large drop of water landed smack-dab on the tip of Lucy's nose. And then another on her forehead. Lucy walked faster. She looked down at the sidewalk, which was quickly darkening with round gray spots.

"I don't even have a jacket," Lucy moaned out loud. "And I'm wearing white!"

She heard a bicycle as it whirred behind her. Seconds later, a cute upperclassman raced by. Lucy had noticed him before at the orientation rally, and she felt her heart rate quicken.

"Nice stripes!" he yelled.

Lucy paled and looked down. She was wearing her red-striped underwear and it was showing through her wet pants. Could this morning get any worse?

The boy looked back and smiled, then raced off. Lucy's face turned bright red.

Great, now my face and my underwear match.

Lucy ducked into the nearest building and realized it was the science hall. She was grateful for one thing as she took refuge in the warm lobby: only science geeks would see her in her candy cane clothing.

She picked up a science journal from the nearest table and held it across her backside as she inspected postings on the lobby corkboard.

Science fairs, Star Trek conventions, lectures on laser technologies, blah, blah, blah . . .

But then a poster caught her eye. A

poster of a young man in a tuxedo dancing with a young woman in a beautiful red gown. It was a poster for the Winter Ball, the biggest formal event of the year. Lucy felt her sadness fade as romantic thoughts consumed her.

Imagine having a dress and a date like that!

Just then, Lucy felt a tap on her shoulder. She turned around and found herself standing face to face with a freckle-faced, redheaded girl. A girl in glasses so thick Lucy could barely make out the color of her eyes. It was Tanya, her neighbor.

"Think we'll ever find a date to the dance?" Tanya squeaked, her voice so soft Lucy had to lean in to hear her.

"What?" Lucy asked.

Tanya stood up straighter, as though preparing to deliver a monologue from a stage. "The dance!" Tanya projected loudly. "Think we'll find dates?"

Lucy shook her head and laughed. Tanya was undoubtedly a quirky girl. "Not at the rate I'm going. It's only two weeks away."

But then something else caught Lucy's eye. She leaned in to read the fine print on the bottom of the poster.

Tanya leaned over Lucy's shoulder, as though she had happened upon a conspiracy. "What's wrong?" Tanya whispered.

Lucy smiled, explaining as she read. "The Winter Ball is a fund-raiser for charities."

Tanya's brow furrowed in confusion. "And . . . ?"

Lucy turned to Tanya. "The Student Council is looking for volunteers to help organize the dance."

Tanya still wasn't sure why this news had perked Lucy up so visibly. "So you're excited because you want some extra work? I can give you some computer codes to hack if you're that bored."

Lucy shook her head, still grinning. "If we get involved, we'll be helping raise money for charity *and* meeting people. *People who may not have dates.*"

Suddenly Tanya's confusion turned to clarity. She nodded, and Lucy noticed that her smile was vibrant and her teeth were as straight and white as an actor's in a toothpaste commercial. She wasn't an unattractive girl underneath those Coke-bottle glasses.

"And even if we don't find dates, we can still have fun," Lucy said, masking her real fear with nonchalance. What if she really *couldn't* find a date?

She shrugged the insecurity off and continued her thought. "Fund-raisers are great. I even know the perfect charity."

Tanya linked her arm in Lucy's and then shook her head vehemently. "Okay, but we're finding dates."

Lucy laughed as she looked outside. The rain was still pouring down. And Lucy was still hungry. Tanya seemed to read Lucy's thoughts.

"Who cares about your pants? Let's eat."

Tanya opened the door and pulled Lucy out into the rain. In seconds, they were squealing and running for the cafeteria.

But now they were armed with a plan. . . .

ISBN: 0-375-81430-2

Note: Due to discrepancies between publishing and television production schedules, content of this excerpt is subject to change in the final printing of *Winter Ball*.

DON'T MISS THIS BRAND-NEW, ORIGINAL 7TH HEAVEN STORY

Now Available!

CAMP
CAMDEN

Lucy and Ruthie are off to summer camp in sunny Malibu, California, where swimming, boating, and horseback riding aren't their only pastimes! Lucy's teaching a class that catches the attention of a handsome counselor, and Ruthie is pulling pranks that make everyone take notice! Meanwhile, back at the Camden house, Simon's trying his latest money-making scheme— day-trading on the Internet! But is the stock market ready for Simon Camden?

Available wherever books are sold!
ISBN: 0-375-81360-8